There was a light at the top of Mount Sangre!

Flickering, rather than steady. Who was up there, and what were they doing? I longed for a better look. Turning on the outside light, I scanned the steps and the yard beyond. There was no one in sight.

Taking a deep breath, I shut off the light, unlocked and opened the front door, and stepped cautiously outside.

As I stared up at Mount Sangre, I heard a faint chanting. From the top? I listened and was sure of it. Though the July night was warm, I hugged myself against an inner chill. There was no doubt in my mind that the chanting and the flickering lights were connected. Reminded of the black candle and the invocation ten years ago, I tasted fear on my tongue.

What dreadful ceremony was being enacted on the bloody hill this night?

Dear Reader,

Welcome once again to Silhouette Shadows. This is only our second month of publication, but the books we have in store for you now and in the months to come are so exciting that I just can't contain my enthusiasm.

Jane Toombs is already well-known to readers of Gothic novels, and with *Return to Bloodstone House* she's about to become a favorite with Shadows readers, as well. This is a contemporary Gothic tale full of mystery and menace and—most of all—the kind of passion that spans the years and lives forever in your memory.

Night Mist, by Helen R. Myers, is a different type of story. It features a ghost, but not your regular sort of ghost. He's . . . well let's just say I'd better not tell you any more or I might give away the secrets you'll enjoy finding out for yourself. I *will* say, though, that those of you who know Helen's work for Silhouette Desire and Silhouette Romance *won't* be disappointed.

In the months to come you can expect to travel regularly to the dark side of love in the company of such terrific and talented authors as Anne Stuart, Terri Herrington, Regan Forest, Patricia Simpson and Lee Karr, not to mention the new stars who'll be coming your way. Plan to shiver your way through the year in the company of Silhouette Shadows, where even the darkest journey always leads to love.

Enjoy!

Leslie Wainger
Senior Editor and Editorial Coordinator

JANE TOOMBS

RETURN TO BLOODSTONE HOUSE

SILHOUETTE® *Shadows*™

Published by Silhouette Books New York

America's Publisher of Contemporary Romance

SILHOUETTE BOOKS
300 East 42nd St., New York, N.Y. 10017

RETURN TO BLOODSTONE HOUSE

Copyright © 1993 by Jane Toombs

All rights reserved. Except for use in any review, the reproduction or utilization of this work in whole or in part in any form by any electronic, mechanical or other means, now known or hereafter invented, including xerography, photocopying and recording, or in any information storage or retrieval system, is forbidden without the permission of the publisher, Silhouette Books, 300 E. 42nd St., New York, N.Y. 10017

ISBN: 0-373-27005-4

First Silhouette Books printing April 1993

All the characters in this book have no existence outside the imagination of the author and have no relation whatsoever to anyone bearing the same name or names. They are not even distantly inspired by any individual known or unknown to the author, and all incidents are pure invention.

® and ™:Trademarks used with authorization. Trademarks indicated with ® are registered in the United States Patent and Trademark Office, the Canada Trade Mark Office and in other countries.

Printed in the U.S.A.

JANE TOOMBS

believes that a touch of the mysterious adds spice to a romance. Her childhood fascination with stories about shape-changers such as vampires, werewolves and shamans never faded, leading to her present interest in supernatural influences, not only in Gothic romances but in the early cultures of all peoples.

A Californian transplanted to New York, Jane and her writer-husband live in the shadow of Storm King Mountain.

CHAPTER ONE

By afternoon, the day grew warm. I'd almost forgotten that June was always very warm in the San Joaquin Valley. I drove past the bobbing pumps of the oil fields, then past full-grown orange trees in groves that had been newly planted ten years ago. The Valencias were in bloom and their sweet perfume invaded the car, banishing the chemical reek of oil.

I was getting close to the foothills now; they loomed ahead of me, cutting off my view of the loftier snow-capped Sierra peaks.

When I turned from the highway onto the two-lane county road that led to the village of Naranada, I glanced over my shoulder at nine-year-old Tibbie, asleep on the back seat. Was I doing the right thing?

If the new owners of the Santa Cruz duplex I was renting hadn't decided to take over my half to live in themselves, I wouldn't be on this road, I wouldn't be returning to Bloodstone House. Ten years ago I'd vowed never to come back.

I shook my head. I was no longer the naive and impressionable eighteen-year-old I'd been then. Besides, sooner or later, I'd have had to return to Naranada and Bloodstone House because, whether I wanted the place or not, three months ago it became mine.

A frisson of fear ran along my spine as I thought about being the last of the Rollands. The end of the line. Like my father, Great-aunt Faith was dead and now there was only me, Valora Rolland. And Tibbie, of course, a Rolland by adoption if not by blood.

I'll only be there for the summer, I told myself firmly. After that, I'll sell the place. Naranada isn't my home; Santa Cruz is.

For Tibbie's sake I'd taken a three-month leave of absence from my job as personnel analyst for the city of Santa Cruz. I'd done everything possible to improve my daughter's health except spend more time with her, so I meant to devote this summer to Tibbie, no matter where we lived.

Naranada never had been my home, except in the summers. From the time I was seven until the year I turned eighteen, I'd spent my summers with Great-aunt Faith at Bloodstone House. I hadn't minded. The isolated old mansion fascinated me and I'd made friends in the village. I enjoyed my summers. Until I turned eighteen.

Stop thinking about that time, I warned myself. What's past is past. Concentrate on Tibbie and the fun she'll have exploring the house.

I wondered if Great-aunt Faith would have enjoyed Tibbie. I realized now she'd been more attached to me than she'd showed when I was with her. Though I hadn't quite managed to love her, despite her abrupt, autocratic and sometimes peculiar ways, I'd been fond of her and I felt guilty about not attending her funeral. But I'd been in Washington, D.C., on a work-related conference and hadn't been notified until too late.

"Are we there yet?" Tibbie spoke sleepily from the back seat.

I tossed her a smile. "Almost. Look, here's the horse ranch I told you about with the iron stallion rearing up by the gate."

Tibbie raised herself and peered at the horse. "Yeah, he really is a stallion. Sometimes they don't put, you know, that male stuff on animal statues."

"We're in ranching country," I told her. "Ranchers take a practical view of animals."

"My great-great-grandfather Rolland was a rancher, wasn't he?"

"He established the first real cattle ranch in Tule Valley. He planted the first orange trees, too. Some of them are still bearing fruit."

"And he built Bloodstone House. What a really neat name. How come you never told me about it until last month?"

I didn't have a good answer. "I guess I never thought about it much." Which was true enough. For ten years I'd done everything I could to wipe the place from my mind.

"And now Bloodstone House is ours." Tibbie rolled the name lovingly on her tongue. "Don't you think it's great to own a house? We never did before. I can hardly wait to see it."

I didn't often lie to Tibbie, but when she'd asked me the origin of the name, I'd made up a story about a bloodstone necklace that had belonged to her twice great-grandmother Rolland. I couldn't bear to speak of the rounded hill behind the house called Mount Sangre, much less the dreadful slab of rock at its top.

"Do any of the kids you played with when you were little still live in Naranada?" she asked.

"I don't know. I imagine most of them have moved away by now."

Travis York might still be there. After all, the York family owned the ranch on the other side of Mount Sangre and had lived in Naranada as long as the Rollands. As for Luis Redhawk—no, I didn't want to think about Luis. Didn't *dare* to might be closer to the truth.

"I was sort of hoping maybe I could be friends with their kids if they did," Tibbie said.

I realized she must be nervous about coming to a strange place where she knew no one, as I'd been when I first arrived here at seven.

"We'll find a way for you to get acquainted," I assured her.

As we drove through the outskirts of town, I glanced back again and saw she was staring dubiously at the rather ramshackle houses we passed, perhaps wondering if Bloodstone House would be the same. Putting myself in her shoes reminded me of how uncertain and frightened I'd been when my mother and stepfather left me with Great-aunt Faith that first summer while they went off to Europe.

"Shall I stop the car so you can get into the front seat with me?" I asked Tibbie.

"Okay." She drawled the word as though it made little difference to her, but the speed with which she scrambled from back to front showed me how much she needed to be physically closer to me at this moment.

I drove through the village, pointing out places I remembered. There were some changes, but essentially Naranada was the same as before—a three-block main street where all the businesses congregated, with the cross streets largely residential. Except for the brick library and village hall, most of the buildings were wooden.

"What's that hill?" Tibbie pointed left toward where the rounded top of Mount Sangre was etched against the afternoon sky.

Sweat dampened my palms; I couldn't bring myself to say its name. "Bloodstone House is just in front of the hill, about two miles from town."

"Does it have a name?" she persisted. Tibbie had a one-track mind when it came to things she wanted to know.

I swallowed and cleared my throat. "Mount Sangre." There, I'd got the words out.

"Sangre." She thought a moment. "That means blood in Spanish, doesn't it?" Without waiting for an answer, she said triumphantly, "I bet the house was named for the hill. Maybe for Great-great-grand-mother's necklace, too, but the hill first." She looked at me. "Why is it called Mount Sangre?"

"No one really knows why the early Spanish settlers named places what they did." I tried to speak casually, having no intention of relating any of the lurid local legends devised to explain the name. I knew very well, though, that eventually someone else in Naranada would tell them to her.

Perhaps it hadn't been such a good idea to return.

I made the familiar turn onto the narrow lane lined by massive valley oaks with faded No Trespassing signs in English and Spanish nailed to them, then the two huge stone pillars joined by the wrought-iron arch loomed before us.

"Look, the letters spell 'Bloodstone House'!" Tibbie cried.

I nodded bemusedly, caught in my own memories of first seeing those iron letters. The gates stood open as they always had, and I drove under the arch between the stone pillars and along the winding driveway flanked by date palms alternating with olive trees. The warm breeze carried the scent of honeysuckle into the car, and I recalled how the tangle of vines climbed trellises to form a shady, perfumed arbor near the barn.

"It smells good here, anyway," Tibbie said, craning her neck to try to catch a glimpse of the house between the trees.

I rounded the last curve and there it was.

"Wow!" Tibbie whispered the word, obviously awed.

Bloodstone House, its gray granite trimmed with wrought iron, rose three stories to a many-chimneyed mansard copper roof. The front was broken only by a multitude of deeply set mullioned windows, and the rounded entry porch reached by three curved stone steps.

As I stopped the car in the inner sweep of the circular driveway, Tibbie unbuckled her seat belt and leaned into the back to retrieve her camera.

"I'm going to take a picture before we go inside," she announced. "Why didn't *you* ever take a picture of the house?"

I shrugged, not caring to admit that ten years ago I'd packed away all my mementos of Naranada, including pictures, and had never touched the box since.

By the time I opened the car's trunk, Jed O'Neill came limping up. "Little Miss Valora," he said, grinning. "Danged if you ain't growed all the way up. Here, let me take them bags for you."

Tibbie drifted over and I introduced her to Jed, who cocked his head and examined her after saying hello. "Well, can't say she looks like anyone 'cepting herself."

Because I'd told my great-aunt whose child Tibbie was when I adopted her, I realized Jed and Delia must know, too. Which meant it was no secret to most of Naranada, not that it made any difference.

And Jed was right—Tibbie didn't resemble her mother.

Jed's limp, I noticed as he walked toward the house with the luggage, was no better or worse than it had been years ago. He'd aged, though—the sun creases around his eyes were now wrinkles and his brown hair had thinned and was sprinkled with gray.

"I don't like it when people talk about me but not to me," Tibbie said in a low tone.

"Jed didn't mean any harm. He's always been outspoken. He worked for Great-aunt Faith all his life. I guess he's been here so long he feels entitled to comment as he pleases about us Rollands."

"But she's dead now so that means he works for you, doesn't it?"

I blinked, taken aback. Of course I realized my great-aunt was dead, but somehow I still expected her to be sitting in the morning room between the dining room and the kitchen, her fingers flying as she tatted while dispensing advice and giving orders.

The only things remaining in the car were Tibbie's backpack and my carryall. I handed her the pack, hefted the carryall and shut the door.

"You left the keys inside," Tibbie observed. "And the door's not locked."

"The keys are so Jed can drive the car into the garage. Don't worry, no one will steal the car. Not here." I doubted that ten years had changed Naranada enough so it wasn't safe to leave the keys temporarily in a car sitting in a private driveway in broad daylight.

The front door was open and Delia, her arms folded under her plump breasts, stood waiting in the entry just as she had the first time I'd entered the house.

"About time you came home," she said in greeting.

The years had changed her very little. Her hair was the same iron gray and her pale blue eyes had lost none of their shrewdness.

"It's good to see you, Delia," I told her, not attempting to respond to what she'd said. "This is my daughter, Tabitha. Tibbie, this is Mrs. Koski."

"I'm Delia to everyone else," she said to Tibbie, "so I might as well be Delia to you, too."

Tibbie smiled at her uncertainly, then resumed staring wide-eyed at the blown-glass chandelier with its dangling crystal beads and prisms.

"I've put the two of you in those connecting rooms you used to have," Delia said. "You remember—to the left of the stairs and down the hall? I won't go up, I'm not as young as I used to be and stairs get to me something sinful."

"Thanks," I said as Tibbie and I climbed the stairs.

Jed had left all the luggage in the larger bedroom, the one I'd always thought of as the rose room because of the wallpaper. I was amazed to find the paper intact and scarcely faded, the red and pink roses still climbing up the walls.

Tibbie took her things through the connecting door into the smaller room. "You've got roses, I've got butterflies," she called to me. "And a roof over my bed."

"A canopy," I told her.

"Whatever. And there's a desk that has a little bookcase with books in it. Mom, they're real old Nancy Drew books—not the paperbacks."

"They were mine," I told her, pausing in my unpacking. "And they are old. When Great-aunt Faith gave them to me she said they'd belonged to her youngest sister."

Charity had died accidentally before she reached twenty. My great-aunt's middle sister, my grandmother Hope, had died young, too, and my father was killed in an accident before he was thirty—before I really knew him. The Rollands had never been a lucky family.

But *I'm* lucky, I told myself fiercely. I've got a wonderful daughter and a good job. And—the thought came unbidden—I've got Bloodstone House.

Tibbie appeared in the doorway with a book in her hand. "I found another book of yours, Mom."

My heart lurched when I saw its dark red cover.

"Something's written inside. 'Happy eighteenth birthday to Valora from Luis.' Who's Luis?"

I reached for the book. "Luis is—was—a boy I used to know." The little volume of verse, light as it was, weighed heavily in my hand, reminding me of things I preferred not to remember.

"Was Luis your boyfriend?"

"No." It was the truth. Whatever had happened between us, Luis had never been my boyfriend. In those days, Travis York had claimed he was. But Luis and me—well, that was different. At the time the difference had frightened me.

Tibbie sat on my bed. "Everything seems different here," she said, echoing the same word I'd used in my thoughts. "Sort of like we came to another country."

"Naranada isn't much like Santa Cruz. Maybe because it's tucked away in the foothills, maybe because most of the people who live here raise beef or grow fruit, maybe because it's so small—or all three."

"Maybe I'll be different, too." Her voice was hopeful.

I had to force myself to be casual. Instead of pulling her into my arms and wrapping them tightly around her in a vain effort to keep her safe from harm, I merely hugged her briefly, ruffled her short brown hair and said, "Maybe."

It was best she didn't know how desperately I prayed this summer would help heal her. That was why we were here—her health was all-important. What did the past matter? The past had no influence over Tibbie, and I refused to allow it to burden me. Hadn't I done everything I could to right the wrong?

When we finished unpacking, we went down the steep back stairs into the kitchen, drawn by the delicious aroma of baking bread. Delia was there, as I knew she would be, sliding a pan of golden-brown rolls from the oven. A younger, fortyish woman was loading the dishwasher. As soon as she turned the rolls onto a towel to cool, Delia introduced us to Mrs. Jennings, who asked to be called Lucy.

"Lucy don't live here. She's strictly day help." Delia went on, "but I might as well admit I couldn't get on without her." She glanced at Tibbie. "I suppose you'll be wanting one of my hot rolls just like—" she paused before finishing with ''—like Miss Valora here used to.''

Tibbie nodded enthusiastically and I gave no indication I knew that Delia had hastily substituted my name for another.

Perched on stools at the kitchen counter, we both ate a roll dripping with butter—never mind the cholesterol or the calories—along with a glass of milk.

''Some things don't change,'' Delia said to me. ''You always did like my rolls and I'm not surprised Tibbie does, either. Been a pile of change around town, though. Hardly anyone you knew lives here anymore except for Travis York. His mother got so she couldn't take the hot summers, so she and his dad moved to Oregon permanently and left Travis to run the ranch.''

''How about Luis?'' Tibbie asked, carefully not looking at me.

''Luis?'' Delia frowned. ''And just how'd you hear about Luis, missy?''

''I saw his name in a book upstairs.''

Delia glanced at me. ''Dr. Redhawk, that's who Luis is these days.''

Tibbie made a face. ''I hate doctors.''

I had difficulty picturing, as an MD, all clinical and proper, the taciturn but fascinating boy I'd known. I waited, expecting Delia to go on, but when she didn't I finally said, ''I suppose Dr. Redhawk doesn't visit in Naranada.''

''He don't need to visit here and that's a fact.''

I bit my tongue to keep from asking why, knowing that's exactly what she wanted. What difference did it make to me what Luis did or didn't do?

"I don't care what you say," Lucy put in, "he's a right good doctor. I go to him so I ought to know."

My heart turned over. Lucy lived in town. If Luis was her doctor that must mean he practiced in Naranada. Lived in Naranada.

"Luis never left the place except to go to college to learn doctoring," Delia said. "Surprised a lot of people, including me, when he made it through and hung out his shingle. 'Family physician' is what he claims he is. Like the York boy, he ain't married yet."

I shot her a barbed glance—she certainly couldn't believe I'd care whether Luis or Travis had married!—but Delia wasn't looking at me. I was tempted to announce that I had no intention of renewing old acquaintances but decided it was best to avoid discussing the subject with her.

Because he lived in town didn't mean I had to see Luis. I'd only be here three months. Surely I could avoid him for that length of time socially. As for medically, I was healthy enough and Tibbie's problem, being specialized, didn't require the care of a general practitioner such as Luis.

Since the York ranch began where the Rolland property ended, sooner or later I'd probably run into Travis. But since he, like Luis, had made no effort to contact me in ten years, he'd surely outgrown his adolescent dream of the two of us ending the ancient York-Rolland feud by marrying each other.

I'd made it absolutely clear at eighteen that I never wanted to have anything to do with either of them for as long as I lived. I'd meant what I said then and I felt little different now. Still, so much time had passed that I could certainly manage to be polite but distant if by chance I had to speak to either of them.

"Are there still horses here?" Tibbie asked while trying to wipe her buttery fingers with a paper napkin.

"Only the one now," Delia said. She glanced at me. "The pony you used to ride. Jed's let her get so fat it's a wonder she can move."

They still had Misty! How I'd loved that gray pony—even when I grew too big to ride her.

"Can we go see the pony right now, Mom?" Tibbie begged.

I jumped off the stool, almost as excited as she was. Opening the pantry door, I noticed the large porcelain sugar bowl with its painted wreath of honeysuckle was still on the bottom shelf. I lifted the lid and removed two of the sugar cubes that my great-aunt always had insisted on buying, believing them far superior to granulated sugar. I handed the cubes to Tibbie as we went through the back door.

When I was ten, my great-aunt finally bowed to the passage of time and had half the barn converted to a garage. Now the doors stood open and I saw that Jed had driven my car inside and parked it next to the gleaming but ancient yellow Rolls that had been Faith's.

Next to the garage was what was left of the original barn. Misty wasn't in any one of the four stalls but in the corral beyond. When Tibbie ran ahead of me and climbed onto the lower rail of the corral fence, Misty ambled over to investigate the stranger.

"Hold the sugar cubes on your palm," I told her. She did and Misty gobbled them up eagerly.

Tibbie giggled, wiping her hand on her jeans. "That tickled."

When no more sugar was offered, Misty turned to me and I stroked her neck, wondering if ponies remembered people after so long a time.

"Can I learn to ride her, Mom?"

"Yes, but not today."

Tibbie sighed. "I know, you want me to rest. Why? I slept practically all the way here in the car."

"You slept for exactly one half hour. Let's take a quick look at the duck pond and then go back to the house. We can explore tomorrow."

We started off along the nearly overgrown path to the duck pond. Again she ran ahead of me until a bend in the path hid her from view. Before I caught up to her, she screamed.

My heart pounding in alarm, I ran as fast as I could. Tibbie sat huddled on the path, sobbing. "My foot, my foot," she cried.

I caught my breath. A two-foot length of weathered board appeared to be glued to the thick rubber sole of her tennies and I feared I knew why. Kneeling beside Tibbie, I pried at the board. She screamed with pain when I pulled it free from her shoe. Blood coated the long, rusted nail protruding from the board.

Gathering her to me, I cuddled her. "You're all right now," I murmured. "All right." But I knew what had to be done before she was really out of danger. So much for avoiding Luis.

When I looked up, Jed was standing over us. He bent down and picked up the board with the nail in it. "Heard the little gal hollering," he said. "Stepped on a nail, did she? Too bad. I'll get rid of this old thing." He started to turn away.

"Wait," I said. "Where's Dr. Redhawk's office?"

He told me and, with me helping her, Tibbie was able to limp to the car. I went into the house to pick up my shoulder bag and then drove into town.

Luis's office was in a bungalow on Dolores Avenue, a block off Sierra, the town's main street. The inside was neither plush nor dingy. *Utilitarian* was as good a word as any. Two older men and one middle-aged woman sat in the waiting room when I brought Tibbie in.

"She stepped on a nail," I told the receptionist. "She's had all her shots but I imagine she'll need a tetanus booster."

"I feel sick to my stomach," Tibbie muttered.

"She looks awfully pale," the receptionist said. "You'd better bring her inside."

Once Tibbie was lying on the examining table, she began to feel better. I took off her shoe and sock, wincing at the sight of the blood oozing from the hole where the nail had gone through the shoe and into the sole of her foot.

Tibbie, watching my face, managed a feeble grin. "You'd never make a nurse, Mom."

I filled out various forms, and the receptionist came in and took them away.

Shortly afterward, the door opened and Luis walked in. He wore a short white doctor's jacket over a T-shirt and chinos. His dark good looks had intrigued me when he was a teenager, and ten years had refined and intensified his attractiveness, leaving me as breathless as if I were still seventeen. He nodded, his gaze flicking over me dispassionately, then fixed his attention on Tibbie in an assessment that took her in from head to foot. His concentration on her left me free to regain my composure.

Tibbie stared at him mistrustfully.

"When I was a kid I punched a hole in my foot with a nail," he told her. "Hurt like the devil."

"Did you have to go to a doctor for a booster shot?" she asked.

"Not exactly. My grandfather was a medicine man so he took care of me." As he spoke, he examined her foot.

"You mean he was a doctor?"

"Nope. A Miwok medicine man." He swabbed the hole with something that foamed white.

Tibbie blinked but didn't protest. "Do you mean he was an Indian?" she asked.

"Right. Like me. So he gathered a lot of different leaves and roots. Some he stewed and some he brewed and some he chewed."

"Chewed!" Caught up in what Luis was saying, Tibbie seemed oblivious to what he was doing to her foot.

"Yes, chewed. Grandfather Running Fox learned all he knew from the medicine man before him—what to brew, what to stew and what to chew. He mixed everything together when it was done, made a poultice and bound it to my foot. Then he did a medicine dance. Since the wound didn't get infected and I didn't get tetanus, he must have done something right, don't you think?" He drew liquid into a syringe from a bottle labeled "tetanus toxoid."

"I guess so."

"I'm still learning things from Running Fox that they didn't teach me in medical school."

"I bet they didn't teach you to chew up stuff there."

"You're right." Deftly he inserted a needle into the skin of her upper arm and injected the solution. By the time she gasped it was all over.

He sat her up. "How do you feel?"

"Better. I guess I'm not going to throw up after all."

"Good. Keep off your foot for the rest of the day and take it easy walking for another day or two, okay? You don't need to come back unless it gets worse instead of better—but I doubt that'll happen." He looked at her for a long moment, then offered his hand. "I'm glad to meet you, Tabitha Faith Rolland."

She gave him her hand and they solemnly shook. "I like being called Tibbie better," she said. "I know I'm supposed to say 'Dr. Redhawk' but I know your first name is Luis 'cause I saw it in a book."

He smiled at her. "In the waiting room?"

"No, in my room at Bloodstone House. You gave the book to my mom a long, long time ago."

I saw him tense before he swung around to look at me. "Valora." He said my name so softly I scarcely heard him.

I couldn't move or speak as his intent gaze trapped me. *Green as mountain ferns* he'd once described my eyes. His were basalt dark, deep and dangerous as a bottomless pool. I could easily drown there, I knew. I almost had once.

The same electrical force crackled between us, a bond time had strengthened rather than weakened, a bond I wanted no part of but was helpless to break free from.

He reached to me and, without my willing it, my hand rose to meet his, hungry for his touch. Wanting, as he'd always made me want, with a frightening urgency only he could evoke.

Before our hands met, he dropped his. Turning abruptly, he strode from the room.

"He's nice," Tibbie said. "Not like a doctor at all. I'm kind of sorry I won't get to see him again. Aren't you sorry, Mom?"

Sorry? Yes. Sorry I'd ever returned to Bloodstone House. And to Luis Redhawk.

CHAPTER TWO

During the next two days, as Tibbie and I settled in and I noticed how she enjoyed exploring the house, I decided I'd made the right choice after all by coming here. Since this summer was Tibbie's, her happiness was more important than any personal reasons I might have had for preferring to be elsewhere.

On the morning of our third day at Bloodstone House, I woke to the sound of a mockingbird singing in a tree outside my open window. A warm breeze carried the faint sweet scent of orange blossoms from a nearby grove. I smiled and stretched, reminded of lazy summer mornings when I was a girl. Though Great-aunt Faith had been a believer in keeping herself and everyone around her busy, my mornings had always been free.

I rose and padded to the open connecting door between the rooms and peered in to see if Tibbie was awake yet. To my surprise, her bed was empty. I frowned, apprehension setting me on edge when I saw her door to the hall was open. Because of her problem, we kept that door locked and she was supposed to go through my room to reach the hall, thus rousing me since I'm a light sleeper. Instead, she'd unlocked her hall door and left that way. Tibbie was usually obedient, so I didn't believe she would have done this if she'd been aware of her actions.

My anxiety rising, I flung on jeans and a T-shirt, slid my feet into sandals and hurried toward the back stairs, calling Tibbie's name.

"No, I never set eyes on the child," Delia told me when I questioned her in the kitchen.

"Me, neither," said Lucy.

Asking Delia to check the downstairs rooms, I sent Lucy upstairs to do the same. I ran outside, hoping against hope Tibbie might have gone to see the pony. But she wasn't in the barn or the corral, where I found Jed.

"Never seen hide nor hair of little Miss Tibbie," he said in answer to my worried question. "Is she missing, then?"

I knew I'd have to explain. "Tibbie has spells where she wanders off—something like sleepwalking. Would you mind helping me look for her?"

"Why, the poor little gal. Be glad to help all I can. Let's see now, you go that way—" he pointed "—and I'll go this'n."

He'd pointed toward Mount Sangre so I hurried toward the base of the hill through a meadow that had been planted to vegetables during my summers at the house. Now grass, weeds and saplings covered the ground. A small, dilapidated storage shed sat in the middle of the meadow, its doorless opening facing the hill. As I approached the shed, I heard a man's voice, vaguely familiar.

"If you won't tell me what you're looking for," he said, "I can't help you find it, can I?"

"Where is it?" Tibbie asked plaintively.

"Can't you say anything else?" the man demanded.

By now I was frantically racing toward the shed. I rounded the corner and saw a blond man blocking the entrance. I couldn't see Tibbie, but I shouted her name.

The man turned and I realized he was Travis York. He smiled at me as I came panting up and reached as though to hug me in greeting, subsiding when I involuntarily raised my hands to hold him away, and merely flicking a strand of my hair with his fingers.

"You're wearing it shorter, but I see your hair's still that bright Rolland red," he said. "I'm glad you've come home, Val. I was walking over to welcome you back to Naranada when I came across—Tibbie, is it?—and I realized she must be your daughter."

He reached inside the shed, put an arm around Tibbie and gently urged her through the doorway. Tibbie, dressed in her nightgown and slippers, stumbled into my arms, her eyes blank as they always were when she had a spell. I held her next to me, knowing she wasn't aware of her surroundings and might wander off if not prevented.

"She didn't seem to know where she was or what she was doing," Travis said. "I was getting ready to bring her to your house when I heard you calling."

"Thank you for finding Tibbie," I said, realizing more was called for but not quite willing to encourage any friendship between Travis and me. "I'd invite you to stop by for coffee but—"

He waved his hand. "But I'd be in the way at the moment. I understand. Tibbie needs peace and quiet. Did I ever tell you I used to sleepwalk myself? I'll wait until after lunch to drop by and officially welcome you home." He smiled again, the same boyish grin I remembered from years past.

In fact, he seemed to hardly have aged, this tall, fair, handsome man who'd once been my friend. I couldn't help but recall the good times we'd had together before that horrible night on Mount Sangre. I bit my lip, concerned about Tibbie and wanting to get her back to the house but uncertain how to dismiss Travis.

He solved my dilemma by saying, "See you later," turning and striding off.

I sighed, now committed to a visit from Travis. So much for avoiding the two men I never wanted to see again.

Keeping my arm around her, I led Tibbie home. She made no resistance; she never did. When we neared the house, Jed saw us and waved, but Tibbie gave no indication she'd noticed him. Or me. Or any of her surroundings.

As we entered the front door, she stopped suddenly, looked around in confusion and said plaintively, "I can't find it." With those words, she came to herself, just as she always did.

Tears welled in her eyes as she glanced at me. "I guess it must have happened again. I'm sorry, Mom."

I hugged her. "It's not your fault."

I called to Delia to tell her Tibbie was with me and took my daughter upstairs to her room. The first thing I did was check her injured foot.

"Where did I go this time?" she asked.

"To a shed on the grounds. A man named Travis York found you there."

"Travis York? The man who lives on the other side of Mount Sangre?" When I nodded, she added, "I heard Delia telling Lucy that he wanted to buy the Rolland estate. Does that mean Bloodstone House, too?"

"Yes," I said, wondering if what Delia had said was true. In the long-ago days when both families first settled in this valley, the Yorks had coveted Rolland land, leading to enmity between them. It hadn't occurred to me Travis might still be interested in Rolland land. My land.

"Please don't sell the house!" Tibbie's plea startled me.

"At the moment I don't have any plans to sell it," I said truthfully.

Tibbie sighed in relief. "Good, 'cause I like it here." She wiggled her toes. "My foot hardly hurts anymore, Mom, it's healing just like Dr. Redhawk told me. I think it's well enough so I can ride Misty."

"We'll see." Her foot did seem to be practically healed. "Wash up, get dressed and we'll go down to breakfast."

While she was getting ready, I locked her hall door and this time pocketed the key. I didn't dare take any more chances on her wandering outside during a spell. God knows there were enough weirdos in the world. What if one of them had found her rather than Travis?

After breakfast, Tibbie, without being reminded, went to the music room to practice her lesson on Great-aunt Faith's rosewood grand piano. Her music teacher in Santa Cruz had given her extra work for the summer and so far her fascination with the ornate piano was keeping Tibbie on schedule.

Feeling Delia and Lucy needed an explanation about Tibbie's problem, I went into the kitchen. Only Delia was there.

"I'd like to talk to you about Tibbie," I said. "She's a perfectly normal child except for these spells that come over her every now and then. One of the doctors I took her to compared them to sleepwalking. She behaves as though she can see what she's doing but, at the same time, she's not aware of what she does. No medication or anything else any doctor has prescribed has stopped her from having them.''

"She looks healthy enough," Delia said. "Her real ma was a mite strange, though, and they do say blood will tell. What's Tibbie make of it all?"

I deliberately ignored the reference to Willa. "I don't think the spells bother Tibbie as much as they do me. I'm always afraid she'll hurt herself, or wander off unseen and be hurt by someone. The only words she ever speaks in a spell are, 'Where is it?' and, when she comes to, 'I can't find it.' "

"Whatever is the poor child looking for?"

"When she's herself she doesn't have the slightest idea what she might be searching for. When she's in a spell she must know but, since she doesn't answer questions then, I've never been able to find out."

"Maybe she'll outgrow them."

I sighed. "I hope so. I thought maybe if I took this summer off to be with her she might improve."

Delia gazed steadily at me. After a moment she nodded, as though making up her mind. "It don't seem to have nothing to do with Tibbie, but did you know your great-aunt spent her last days and nights wandering around searching?"

I stared at her. "Searching for what?"

"She said something about a book and that put me in mind of the old family book you lent to Travis York all those years ago. I thought he must have given the book back, but I wasn't sure so I finally told her what you done.

"'I've burned the book,' she snaps at me, 'but where's what came out of the book? I had it once and now it's gone. The owl calls to me, you know. Why can't I find it?'" Delia shook her head. "She wouldn't come right out and tell me what she couldn't find but I think I know. Ten years ago she sent Jed up Mount Sangre to look for something and he'd brought back a silver medallion."

A frisson of fear slithered along my spine as I realized what Delia had described. The owl medallion Travis had used on that terrible night.

"Do you know what she did with that medallion?" Delia asked.

I shook my head.

"My idea is, she hid it herself and when she got forgetful, she couldn't recall where." Delia frowned. "The search killed her in the end, her prowling through the house every night, old as she was and with a bad heart. I heard a noise early one morning, found she wasn't in her bed, came down and there she was sprawled on her face on the library floor. She died in my arms."

"I—I had no idea." I'd assumed she'd died peacefully in bed. Tears pricked my eyes. "I'm sorry."

"So you well might be. You never should have lent out the book that medallion came in, without her permission, when you knew how Miss Faith felt about family things."

Feeling justly chastised, I bowed my head. It was bad enough that I'd known how possessive my great-aunt had been about what she owned yet still had allowed Travis to take that awful old book. But I never dreamed what horror would follow. To discover my thoughtlessness had also helped to cause her death was a bitter blow.

"It's all water under the bridge now," Delia said. "No amount of regret brings back the dead."

How well I knew. Indirectly that terrible book had killed Willa, too. And it had been my fault.

Tibbie burst into the kitchen. "I played 'Country Gardens' all the way through without one single mistake. Did you hear?"

I shook my head. Firmly putting the past aside, I forced a smile and said, "I think one good lesson deserves another, though. If you'll change those shorts for jeans, we'll ask Jed to saddle Misty."

Bouncing with delight, Tibbie ran up the back stairs.

"She don't seem none the worse for that spell, does she?" Delia asked.

"They don't seem to harm her. I forgot to mention that Travis York found her. He'll be calling here after lunch."

Delia raised her eyebrows but made no comment.

Tibbie's feet pounded on the wooden back stairs announcing that she'd changed in record time. We left the house to find Jed and Misty.

Though the pony ambled around the corral at a snail's pace with me leading her, Tibbie was thrilled with her first ride, insisting that by tomorrow she'd be ready to ride without me being on lead. As lazy as Misty had gotten, it would probably be perfectly safe to allow Tibbie to try but I didn't promise anything.

Travis arrived after two. I was playing old maid with Tibbie in the morning room and Travis immediately demanded to be dealt into the game. He soon had

Tibbie giggling at his obvious ploys to get rid of the old maid card.

"You can't be an old maid anyway 'cause you're a man," she informed him.

"How about an old bachelor?" he asked.

Tibbie shook her head. "Doesn't count."

By the time we finished the third game, with me a three-time loser, I had to admit I enjoyed Travis's company just as much as I had in the past. I'd completely forgotten how charming he could be.

"My mom isn't really an old maid," Tibbie explained to him. "She's a single parent."

Travis winked at me. "Maybe she won't be forever."

Tibbie thought it over. "I'd sort of like a father, but it's okay just to have Mom."

I blinked. Never before had Tibbie indicated she missed having a father. Perhaps she found Travis charming, too. The thought upset me so much I paid scant attention when she invited him to listen to her play "Country Gardens." As I trailed after them to the music room, the past clouded my mind, tarnishing the easy camaraderie I'd reestablished with Travis.

Because I could never be sure.

After he left, I settled Tibbie with a book on her bed to rest—she'd risen far too early—and hurried off to the kitchen where Delia was preparing the evening meal.

"After you mentioned Willa earlier," I said, striving to sound casual, "I got to wondering what became of the biker she used to date."

"That no good Jack Norton, you mean? He joined the navy and never came back to town. Good riddance, that's what I say." She looked up from the pie crust she was rolling out to give me a shrewd glance. "Could've been him, that's for sure."

Yes, it could have been. But I couldn't forget there were two other possibilities.

Delia lowered her voice. "What'd you tell Tibbie?"

"She knows that both her birth mother and her father are dead," I said firmly, ignoring Delia's raised eyebrows. What else could I have told my daughter? At least it was half the truth.

Tibbie went to bed at nine and almost immediately fell asleep. Since she'd never had a spell at night, nor two spells close together, I felt confident enough to leave the house after telling Delia I wanted to take a walk on the grounds.

I strolled though the soft darkness, passing a grape-stake fence where night-blooming jasmine climbed, its starry white blossoms perfuming the air and reminding me of long-ago summer nights at Bloodstone House. I'd been as romantic a teenager as most girls and had enjoyed pretending I was a glamorous femme fatale on my way to meet a secret lover in the quaint Victorian gazebo that overlooked the duck pond. Enjoyed pretending until—

I shook my head. Enough of the past. As Delia had insisted, water under the bridge. Gone. Unrecoverable. Which was just as well.

Though I hadn't meant to go to the gazebo, I was irresistibly drawn to the graceful octagonal building with its open sides. I climbed the rise, then the steps, found the built-in seats still intact and sat down, gazing at the waxing moon's reflection in the water of the pond. In the country the night is never silent but filled with the piping of frogs and the chirr of nocturnal insects. Restful sounds, these, far different from the distraction of city noises.

I relaxed as I listened, soothed into dreaminess. Why had I forgotten the many wonderful days I'd spent at Bloodstone House? Surely I'd been right to return.

Without my willing it, Luis's image came into my mind. Not as I'd seen him a few days ago, but as the twenty-year-old he'd been ten years before, stripped to the waist, wearing ancient faded jeans molded to his body.

Perhaps because of his Native American heritage, he had little hair on his chest except right in the center where a few black whorls curled between his nipples. For some reason I tingled all over when I caught a glimpse of his bare chest.

"He's got the corner on sexy," I remember my friend Corenna whispering to me once when she saw him working on the grounds. "If he stared at me like he does you I'd melt into a puddle right here on the grass."

"He doesn't stare at me!"

"Ha! He's doing it right now—you're just too chicken to look back at him."

"What, and melt into a puddle? No, thanks."

Corenna had gone into a fit of giggles, letting me off the hook. I'd been well aware of and secretly thrilled by how Luis's dark gaze often followed me when he worked in the Rolland gardens, but I hardly admitted it to myself, much less my girlfriends. Besides, that summer I was sort of going steady with Travis York. At least Travis thought so.

Actually, I liked Travis a lot, but he never made me feel the strange, rather frightening warmth deep inside me that Luis evoked whenever our glances met.

Nothing more had come of it because, as Corenna correctly guessed, I was not only too inexperienced to realize what my response meant, but I was also afraid of the way Luis could make me feel without even touching me. I'd let Travis kiss me a dozen or so times and liked it, but I'd never felt so much as a tingle. So Travis was safe for me. Luis was not.

But then one July night, a night like this, silvered with moonlight and scented by jasmine, I had come to the gazebo, one of my favorite private places, so private I'd never taken any of my friends there, not even Travis. I sat and watched the fireflies twinkling like stars among the bushes and conjured up an image of my dream lover. More and more he was beginning to resemble Luis and this disturbed me.

On that well-remembered night, I rose and walked to the rail, lifting my face to the moon, closing my eyes as I let its silver light wash over and through me, sensing an indefinable magic in the soft breeze that stirred wisps of my hair. In my moonlit reverie I was the most beautiful and desirable woman in the world and there was only one man perfect enough to be my love. This man walked toward the gazebo, toward me, on a silver path; he was close, closer, and when I opened my eyes, he'd be standing beside me.

I opened my eyes and was astounded. There he was! His arms reached for me and, in a daze, I stepped into his embrace and into a searing kiss that branded my very soul with his name.

Though still wrapped in my fantasy, on another level I was aware it was Luis who held me, whose lips kissed mine. It was Luis's silky dark hair under my fingers, his body pressed close to mine. This was what I'd wanted from him all along, feared and longed for at the same time. Corenna was right; I was melting, melting, becoming a part of him, and I found the sensation glorious.

Until he stopped kissing me, stopped caressing me and backed away. "If I touch you again I won't be able to stop." His strange raspy voice excited me. I didn't want him to stop, not ever.

"Not like this," he said. "It's not fair to you. Not right."

"I don't care," I whispered, hungry for his touch.

"Maybe not now but you will later." His finger brushed my lips, making me gasp for breath. "Valora, my love," he'd murmured. "Don't forget me." And then he was gone, taking my heart with him.

I blinked, coming back to the here and now—it was June, not July, and I was twenty-seven, not seventeen. But some things never change.

"I knew I'd find you waiting here for me," Luis said from behind me.

I sprang up and uneasily watched him climb the steps into the gazebo. He wore chinos, not jeans, and a shirt that buttoned instead of a T-shirt. Otherwise he looked as dangerously desirable as ever.

"I—I wasn't waiting for you," I said, the quaver in my voice betraying my pounding heart.

He looked at me, telling me without words that we both knew better. Without willing it, I found myself gliding into his embrace as I'd done ten years ago.

Though I was no longer seventeen, his kiss devastated me in the same way it had then. The only difference was that this time I managed to pull away before I melted.

He immediately stepped back. "That's probably wise," he said, "since you ought to leave Naranada as soon as possible."

I stared at him, still enmeshed in the passion evoked by his kiss. "Leave?"

"You and Tibbie both. Whatever possessed you to bring Willa's daughter back here?"

His question shattered the spell he'd cast over me. What business was it of his that I'd chosen to spend the summer here?

"I own Bloodstone House," I said coolly. "I have a perfect right to bring my child here."

"I know you inherited the place—who else did the old woman have to leave it to?—but I thought you had more sense than to return."

"It's only for a few months. Besides, what right do you have to tell me what to do?"

"No right," he said, "no right at all. But anyone is free to give advice. Mine is to pack up and take yourself and Tibbie back to Santa Cruz before anything happens."

"Happens?" My voice rose with my annoyance. "What do you mean? Why are you trying to frighten me?"

"I don't know about you but I spent the worst few hours of my life on top of Mount Sangre ten years ago. Make no mistake, what we woke that night is still there. Waiting. You know what happened to Willa. Why endanger Tibbie?"

"Tibbie won't be going anywhere near that rock! I've already made up my mind not to let her climb Mount Sangre."

He snorted derisively. "Will you be able to keep Tibbie from doing what she wants to do? If she's like most kids it'll only whet her interest."

I swallowed, suddenly afraid. Is that where Tibbie had been heading when I found her in the shed this morning? Even if she obeyed me while she was herself, neither she nor I had any control over what she might do when overcome by one of her spells.

"What could possibly harm her during the day?" I demanded, changing tactics. "What happened to the four of us was at night. And the worst of it could have been due to the storm."

"What happened wasn't the storm's doing and you know it. Make no mistake—you and Tibbie are in danger as long as you stay at Bloodstone House. If I wasn't damn sure that was true, why in hell would I be telling you to leave town when I've just found you again?"

"What do you mean 'found me again'? You've just told me to go back to Santa Cruz—obviously you've known all along where I lived, so how could I be lost? You could have come to see me at any time."

"To what purpose? You made it very clear you never wanted to set eyes on me again. 'As long as I live' were your exact words. Would you have welcomed me?"

I shook my head. At the time I was unwilling to face either Travis or Luis. Afraid.

"Then why should I have made us both miserable by trying to force myself on you?" he demanded.

"Damn it, you shouldn't have come back. Naranada is my home. They need me here. But it's no place for you. Or Tibbie."

I thought of the Miwok families scattered over the nearby hills and valleys, most of them poverty-stricken. Luis had come back to take care of his people and they did need him. They needed health care desperately. Naranada wasn't my home; it never would be. To make the kind of money I needed to raise Tibbie, I had to live in or near a community large enough to provide opportunities in my chosen field—personnel.

Yet I didn't want Luis to be right about my having to leave here. I didn't want him to be right about anything, including the fact I undoubtedly would have refused to have anything to do with him if he'd approached me while I was a university student at Santa Cruz. Especially after Willa died.

"It's true I didn't care to be reminded of what happened on Mount Sangre," I said defensively. "You can hardly blame me for not wanting you to come anywhere near me. But how could you be so sure that, given time, I might not change my mind? In ten years you didn't once try to contact me. One letter would hardly have meant a lifetime commitment."

I knew I was being unreasonable but I didn't care. Luis's touch had disinterred a long-buried passion I didn't want to feel again, a passion I didn't even dare to acknowledge.

He didn't reply in words. Instead his hands gripped my shoulders and his mouth came down hard on mine in a kiss that held no tenderness, a kiss that was all hot demand, a kiss that sizzled along my nerves, making me wish it could last forever.

And then, as he'd done years before, he let me go abruptly and strode away, leaving me aching with frustrated need.

"Damn you, Luis," I muttered. "Damn, damn, damn."

CHAPTER THREE

All was darkness except for a tiny golden glow that illuminated Willa's pale face. I saw that the glow came from the cat's-eye ring she wore on her left hand, the ring I had given her long ago. But Willa was dead.

She smiled sadly. "Valora, come with me."

As the darkness lightened into the gray of evening, we walked together in an orange grove, Willa and I, her black kitten with the white mask scampering along beside us. Despite the seeming peacefulness, fear soured my mouth and the soft breeze stirring the green leaves surrounding us did nothing to warm my inner chill. When at last I tried to warn Willa that danger lurked in the gathering dusk, I couldn't speak.

Suddenly, in a silent swoop, the white owl that haunted the groves pounced on the kitten, grasping it in his cruel talons and winging up and away, leaving the death cry of the little cat echoing in my ears.

I turned to Willa and found I was alone. From high in the ancient sycamore growing beyond the grove came the owl's mournful hooting. Four times it called.

"The snowy owl warns of death," Great-aunt Faith whispered.

I whirled but, though I could smell her sweet and heavy lily-of-the-valley scent, I couldn't see my great-aunt.

*"The hummingbird is drawn to red. Bloodred." I
didn't understand what she meant but her eerie whisper sent shivers along my spine.*

*Before darkness overwhelmed me, I felt a silken
feather between my fingers.*

I woke in panic and searched frantically for my
bedside lamp. Once I flicked the light on, I stared at
the roses climbing the walls, hugging myself as I sat
bolt upright on my bed, trying to reassure myself that
I was alone and safe in my own room.

In my imagination I could still see the ominous
swoop of the dream owl, its white wings spread and its
talons outstretched. Ten years ago, it had been no
dream. Willa and I had walked at dusk in the groves
with her kitten and, horrified, had seen it snatched
from us by the owl.

The image shifted, becoming a white enameled owl
etched onto metal, more deadly and malevolent than
its live counterpart. I realized I was visualizing the
medallion, the owl medallion that Travis had found in
that terrible old book. Great-aunt Faith had told Delia she'd burned the book, but what had she done with
the medallion? *The owl calls to me,* she'd said to Delia. What had she meant?

Had she believed in the superstition that an owl
calling a person's name meant death? Did she fancy
she heard her name in the hooting of the snowy owl
that hunted in the the orange groves? Or had Greataunt Faith been searching for the owl medallion when
she died?

Travis had returned the book after that horrible
night ten years ago but not the medallion, claiming
he'd lost it. Delia claimed Jed had recovered the me-

dallion for Great-aunt Faith. Where was it now? I shuddered, shaking my head, wishing I could shake it hard enough to rid my mind of the dreadful memories.

A spot of green on the white candlestick bedspread caught my eye and I reached for it, gasping when I found myself holding a tiny iridescent green feather—a hummingbird feather. At the same time I thought I caught a faint whiff of lilies of the valley.

You had a dream, I told myself firmly. A dream of the past. But that didn't explain the reality of the feather in my hand.

The dream had begun with the gleam of the cat's-eye ring I'd so impulsively given Willa when she'd turned nineteen a month before my own eighteenth birthday. I remembered that I'd been in my room sorting through the contents of the ebony jewel case my mother had sent me when Willa tapped at my bedroom door and I called to her to come in....

"I didn't mean to disturb you," she said, "but Miss Faith asked me to remind you about the library."

"Tell her Travis is coming over in the morning to help me get started on the books." As Willa turned to leave, I motioned her closer.

Since Willa was the only one at Bloodstone House at all near my age, I often confided in her. Great-aunt Faith didn't entirely approve of my being so familiar—Willa was a servant, so therefore, to her way of thinking, not an appropriate friend for me. But I found Willa's obvious admiration flattering even if it did make me a bit uneasy.

"Come look at what my mother sent," I said, gesturing for her to sit next to me on the bed. "She finally decided I was old enough to be trusted with the

jewelry my father left to me." I fingered a man's ring
of black onyx set with four small diamonds, wishing I
knew more about my father. He'd died when I was
three, too young to have more than the vaguest of
memories of him.

"What kind of jewel is that beautiful glowing one?"
Willa asked, pointing to another, smaller ring with a
smoky golden stone.

Knowing little about gems, I shrugged, more interested in winding the gold pocket watch to see if it still
ran.

"Do you mind if I try on the ring?" Willa asked
hesitantly.

Holding the watch to my ear, I replied absently, "Be
my guest."

After a time I noticed how longingly Willa stared at
the ring she'd slid onto her fourth finger. The gold-
colored stone held no particular appeal for me and I
wondered at her enthrallment.

"Don't you think this is too small to have been your
father's?" she asked finally.

Looking at her slender fingers, I nodded. "Maybe
it was his mother's—my grandmother Hope's, I mean.
She was my great-aunt's sister. My grandfather was
also named Rolland—he was a distant cousin of the
Rollands that settled here."

Willa sighed wistfully, caressing the stone with her
forefinger. "This is doubly a family heirloom, then."

Willa had been orphaned at twelve and taken in by
my great-aunt when no relatives could be found. Since
Faith believed everyone should earn their keep, she'd
trained Willa as her housemaid.

I may have lost my father, but I did have blood relatives—my mother and Great-aunt Faith. I also had a stepfather who was kind though distant. Compared to Willa I had lots of family. But, since I'd never seen it before, the ring meant little to me. I didn't consider it an heirloom, single or double.

"Please keep it," I said impulsively.

Willa's eyes opened wide. "Keep the ring? Oh, Valora, you can't mean it. Why, this must be worth all kinds of money."

I smiled at her. "Your birthday's next week so that's my present for you."

She flung her arms around my neck and hugged me, then leaped to her feet and twirled around the room, her hand held out so she could admire the ring. "I love it, I love it," she trilled. "I never expected to own anything so pretty."

At that moment, with her fair hair fanned out and her thin face animated, Willa looked radiantly pretty herself and I told her so.

She flushed. "I'm not, really. Jack keeps telling me I look like a scared rabbit."

I didn't think much of Jack Norton. Despite the macho way he swaggered around in his biker's leathers, he reminded me of a ferret. Great-aunt Faith didn't approve of him, either, so Willa had to sneak out at night to meet Jack.

"I just know my entire life is going to change now that I have this ring," Willa had added. "And I owe it all to you."

Sitting here on my bed ten years later, it hurt me to recall her words. Yes, Willa's life *had* changed drastically. But what she owed to me was her death.

The bad dream, along with my memories of the past, convinced me I wasn't likely to fall asleep again easily. To banish my morbid thoughts, I decided to read. Placing the green feather on my bedside stand, I picked up a book and found myself holding Luis's gift, the only one he'd ever given me, *The Ghost Walkers* by Rozana Webb.

I'd left it here at Bloodstone House, wanting no reminders of my eighteenth birthday. Opening the thin volume now, I flipped through it, glancing at the poems. I'd never heard of the author, which wasn't surprising because poetry was never my thing. Luis, I decided, had chosen this book because the poet wrote about Indians.

Words caught my attention; I paused, hair rising on my nape as I read,

> "How soft the wind blows
> Where the dead walk the sundown
> ... We've heard The-Death-Owl.
> In the land beyond sunsleep..."

I closed the book with shaking hands, feeling as though the writer had shared my unpleasant dream. I feared I might discover even more ominous lines if I read on. I wished I were a child again and could seek comfort by crawling into my mother's bed, but I was grown, with a child of my own to look after, and I had no one to turn to for comfort.

Not Luis. Nor Travis. Never. Because they'd been on Mount Sangre ten years ago and so I could never be sure....

I was still awake when dawn turned the clouds rosy but left my mind as shadowed as ever. My gloom didn't lift until Tibbie woke and tiptoed into my room.

"Jed promised he'd give me a riding lesson this morning," she announced when she saw I was awake, "so I want to be ready." She picked up the green feather. "Where did you get this?"

I improvised. "It might have come out of one of those old books." For all I knew, perhaps it had. I certainly didn't believe Great-aunt Faith had given the feather to me in a dream.

Holding the feather, she danced around the room singing, "I like it here, I like it here," reminding me of Willa with the cat's-eye ring. As had the owl medallion, the ring had disappeared during that dreadful night on Mount Sangre.

"If you want to be ready on time, you'd better get dressed." I spoke more sharply than I meant to, but Tibbie didn't seem to notice.

She scampered into her room, dropping the green feather onto my bed as she passed. I lifted it gingerly, tucked it into the drawer of the old-fashioned nightstand and rose, feeling as though I was ready to pack up and leave Bloodstone House. Yet it wouldn't be fair to Tibbie. She was obviously enjoying herself and she'd be crushed if I took her away so abruptly.

The danger, I told myself firmly, is all in the past. There's nothing here to harm you or your daughter, not anymore.

Once breakfast was over and Tibbie had gone with Jed to ride the pony, I entered the library, determined to keep myself busy so I'd have no time for gloomy thoughts. Delia had told me that Great-aunt Faith never had completed the cataloging of the family books that I'd begun as a teenager, so now I meant to finish what I'd started.

Wearing ancient jeans and a decrepit UC Santa Cruz T-shirt, I disinterred the old files from the cupboard under the windows and sorted through them to discover what had been left undone.

I was perched on an upper rung of the book ladder, checking the books on the top shelf, when a title caught my eye: *The Lore of Gemstones*. I eased the book free and looked up cat's-eye. After discovering it was an opalescent variety of quartz or chalcedony, which meant little to me, I read on. "The belief exists that this semiprecious stone is attuned to earth and to nature and may act as a transmitter of energy."

Whatever that meant. I was sliding the book back into place when Travis's voice startled me.

"Val on the ladder," he said. "Now that's a familiar position. Find anything interesting?"

I started to smile in greeting, but his last few words aborted it. *Find anything interesting?* was the very same question he'd asked the last time we were together in this library.

I'd replied, "Weird, anyway," as I handed an old and battered calfskin-bound book down to him. And that had been the beginning. . . .

"Val?" I suddenly realized Travis had been repeating my name.

"I was remembering." Somberness tinged my words.

He crossed to the foot of the ladder. "Remembering accomplishes nothing. Hell, the past is dead and gone. Didn't anyone ever tell you the present is the best place to live? In case you haven't noticed, this is turning out to be one damned hot day. I came over to invite you and Tibbie for a swim."

Though Great-aunt Faith had always insisted a swimming pool was a waste of money, the Yorks felt different and had a gorgeous pool built into their patio. I'd enjoyed that pool as a teenager and the idea of a swim appealed to me now.

"Tibbie loves to swim," I said. "Sometimes I think she's got a mermaid gene or two."

"Round her up and let's go!"

Travis was right, I decided as the three of us, in his pickup, bounced over the rutted dirt road that connected the two ranches. Not only was this a perfect day to be poolside but, since I'd returned to Bloodstone House, I'd spent far too much time reliving the past.

"I won the freestyle in our last school meet," Tibbie was saying to Travis.

"Did your mother ever tell you I once tried out for the Olympic swim team?" Travis asked.

Tibbie shook her head, staring up at him admiringly. "You must be really, really good."

He shrugged. "Good but not the best. At least in swimming." He smiled, more to himself than at either of us.

I noted that secret smile, wondering if he smiled like that when all the high school girls used to chase him. From what Delia said, I gathered he was still the most sought-after bachelor in town. Why not? Travis was a hunk, no doubt about that, and a wealthy rancher besides.

"Can I ask you a question?" Tibbie said to him.

He grinned at her. "Anything within reason."

"My mom says you have a great big ranch of your own so I was wondering why you wanted to buy Bloodstone House."

Travis's grin faded and he shot me a quick glance.

"Tibbie," I began, "that's Mr. York's business. He—"

"Never mind," Travis cut in. "I don't mind answering. Just give me a minute to think where to start. I suppose you're too young to know much of Shakespeare, Tibbie, but maybe you've heard of *Romeo and Juliet*."

"Sort of."

"You know what a feud is? Well, Romeo was a Montague, Juliet was a Capulet and they fell in love even though their two families hated each other. A long time ago the Yorks and the Rollands quarreled over land. My great-grandfather believed he owned Mount Sangre and Valora's great-grandfather insisted the hill was legally his. The court finally ruled Mount Sangre belonged to the Rollands, but my York ancestor swore to his dying day that the judge was bribed by a Rolland."

"That's not true!" I protested.

"Whether it is or not," Travis went on, "the Yorks never forgave the Rollands, not until I met Valora. We had a teenage romance just like Romeo and Juliet and I decided the way to end the feud once and for all was for us to get married. Valora thought we were too young."

"Your proposal was no more than a joke," I sputtered, aware he was making more of our teenage relationship than it deserved. I hesitated to argue, because I didn't like Tibbie being involved, but I did add, "You weren't serious."

"Ah, but I was. You were the one who laughed, not me."

"You weren't serious," I repeated, determined to keep things the way I'd perceived them at seventeen.

"And this is a lot of nonsense. The Yorks and Rollands never actually feuded."

"We have a family journal that records the time your great-grandfather took a potshot at mine and clipped off his earlobe."

Tibbie had been looking from one to the other of us, fascinated. Fixing her gaze on Travis, she said slowly, "So if you bought Bloodstone House the Yorks would own Mount Sangre."

"Something like that," he agreed.

"My mom told me she isn't ever going to sell."

That wasn't exactly what I'd said, but I wound up nodding. God knows, I hated Mount Sangre and found the idea of owning it repulsive, but somehow the thought of selling the hill made me uneasy.

"I should think you'd want to be rid of that bloody place," Travis said to me.

Since there was nothing I'd like more, I remained silent.

Travis laughed. "I guess the only thing left to do is to marry your mother, Tibbie, and combine the York-Rolland properties."

"First she has to say yes," Tibbie reminded him.

Both of them looked expectantly at me and I shrugged and glanced away, drawing in my breath when a small, dark animal darted in front of the truck, barely missing being run down. A rabbit? A cat?

"Keep your eyes on the road," I warned him. "You almost hit that animal. And hear this! I don't want another word said about the Yorks or the Rollands or anything connected with them, including the three of us."

"But, Mom," Tibbie began, then bit her lip and subsided, to my relief.

We rode in silence until Travis pulled into his driveway, lined by tall Canary Island pines. From her seat between us, Tibbie peered through the windshield at the trees. Suddenly she pointed.

"There's a great big white bird perched up almost at the top of that tree," she said. "What is he?"

Being taller, neither Travis nor I could see the tops of the pines but it seemed he didn't have to.

"I expect he's the snowy owl that hunts at night in our citrus groves," he said. "There've always been white owls at the ranch—it's a family tradition."

Tibbie noticed my grimace. "Don't you like owls, Mom? We learned about them in science class and I think they're neat." A moment later she was distracted by her first sight of the York mansion in all its gingerbread and cupola glory. "Wow," she breathed, much as she had when she saw Bloodstone House.

I didn't blame her. The three-story frame Victorian house, blindingly white in the bright sunshine, was not only a memorial to another era but an architectural nightmare. Truly one of a kind.

Tibbie and I changed into our suits in one of the cabanas near the pool and enjoyed an hour's swim with Travis. Later, the housekeeper-cook served the three of us a salad lunch at an umbrella table on the patio. Tibbie, fascinated by the green-and-yellow parakeet twittering at us from a cage hanging on the fruitless mulberry shading the patio, asked its name.

"I'm not sure," Travis said. "My mother left her behind when they moved to Oregon, because she was convinced the bird would miss the valley. I think of the parakeet as Iphigenia."

"That's a hard name to say," Tibbie observed.

"But it fits her." Again I noticed his secret smile.

After Travis drove us home, Tibbie, tired from the pony ride and the swim, made no objection when I suggested she go upstairs and rest for an hour. Once she'd left us alone in the entry of Bloodstone House, I faced Travis.

"I don't want you talking to Tibbie about the past," I told him.

"Why not?" he demanded. "She's old enough to understand and it's no secret the Yorks and the Rollands have been longtime foes."

"Please do as I ask." I spoke sharply, refusing to argue.

He shrugged, smiled and said, "Overprotective, aren't you?"

I didn't reply.

"But then," he went on, "maybe you should be, considering."

"Considering what?" I snapped defensively.

"Well, the sleepwalking. And then Willa wasn't any too healthy, was she?"

I took a deep breath, trying not to be hostile, aware I tended to overreact to any criticism of Tibbie and resenting his mention of Willa, who'd been healthy enough until after that night on Mount Sangre.

"The, uh, sleepwalking *is* a problem," I admitted.

"Don't worry—I outgrew mine and she will, too." He lifted his hand as though to touch me and, without thinking, I stepped back. Grinning ruefully, he said, "I enjoyed our swim and I promise to discuss only the weather and the price of oranges on our next outing. Am I forgiven?"

It had always been difficult to stay angry with Travis. I returned his smile, he gave me a quick salute and left.

Should there be a next outing? I asked myself as I climbed the stairs. It was true Tibbie seemed to like Travis and she'd certainly appreciated his pool, but was it wise for me to see him again? I was still pondering this when I reached my room.

"Mom," Tibbie called through the open connecting door, "I've been wondering about something. Actually two things."

When I entered, she was propped against the pillows on her bed, a book beside her. "Why does Mr. York call his mom's parakeet by that funny name? What does the name mean?"

I thought back to my college courses in mythology. "Let's see, in Greek mythology, if I remember correctly, Iphigenia was the daughter of a great chieftain and he was forced to sacrifice her in order to win a war."

Tibbie grimaced. "Kill her, you mean?"

"I'm afraid so. They seemed to do a lot of that in the old myths."

"I think it's a dumb idea."

"I'm not arguing. What's your other question?"

"It's about my birth mother. Did Mr. York know her?"

I nodded and sat down next to her. "Naranada is a small town, sweetie, lots of people knew Willa."

"Dr. Redhawk, too?"

"Yes. Why do you ask?"

Tibbie frowned. "I guess it's because I never before met anyone who knew her—'cept you. Do you think Dr. Redhawk or Mr. York would mind if I asked him what she was like?"

I took a deep breath and let it out slowly. Tibbie must never even suspect the truth! "I've told you about Willa," I reminded her.

"Yes, but you always say the same things. They might say something different. 'Specially Dr. Redhawk. When you ask him a question he really listens. And maybe—maybe they'd know more about my father than you do."

"No!" Immediately realizing I'd spoken far too vehemently, I tried to cover the lapse. "I was Willa's best friend so I don't think anyone knows any more about your father than I do."

"But you don't really know anything, not even his name. All you can tell me is he's dead like she is."

My face must have revealed my distress, because Tibbie hunched closer and hugged me. "Don't be sad," she said. "You're the best mom in the world so I don't really care if I never know who my father is."

What I couldn't tell her was that I knew her father was one of three men—and that, since I'd brought her to Bloodstone House, she'd met two of the three.

CHAPTER FOUR

After a restless night, once more plagued with dreams where phantasms spoke in riddles, I roused to find a feather on my bed, a black feather. Over the quilled end was attached a shorter feather, red, tipped with a narrow band of yellow. Echoing in my mind I heard the dream voice of my aunt: *The red-winged blackbird carries a threat of death.*

Shuddering, I slid the feather into the drawer with the other. The first feather might have been a coincidence, but I couldn't convince myself this second one was. But how had the feathers gotten onto my bed?

No one slept inside the house at night except Delia, myself and Tibbie. I couldn't imagine the stout and aging Delia creeping into my room to deliver feathers while I slept. As for Tibbie, she'd never been a secretive child. If anything, she was too blunt and outspoken.

An intruder? I was and always had been a light sleeper; it was well-nigh impossible to believe someone had broken into the house and come upstairs to my room without awakening me. And to what purpose? To leave feathers? I also found it impossible to believe that Great-aunt Faith's ghostly hand had placed the feathers on my bed. Ghosts were pure superstition; I refused to believe in the occult.

Troubled by what had happened, I waited until after breakfast to approach Delia in the kitchen, when Tibbie went off with Jed to ride Misty, and Lucy was occupied with vacuuming the entry.

Because I wasn't quite certain how to start, I began by mentioning that I'd had a bad dream about the time the white owl had killed Willa's kitten.

"I remember that kitten was from one of Sombra's litters," Delia said. "She had four kittens once a year, regular as clockwork, till Miss Faith had her spayed. Most always one of the kittens was marked like her— black with a white face."

Sombra had been my great-aunt's cat. "I suppose Sombra finally died of old age," I said.

Delia shook her head. "She was getting on all right enough, but there wasn't much wrong with her. She up and disappeared the same night Miss Faith died. Never found hide nor hair of her. Kind of gave me the creeps, it did."

"I'm sure you still lock the doors every night just as you did when Great-aunt Faith was alive," I said, knowing I was being abrupt but eager to get to my real reason for talking to her.

Delia blinked. "'Course I do! Don't leave windows open, neither. Miss Faith never held with it when she was alive and I don't see no reason to do different now that she's dead and gone."

"I agree that it's a good idea," I said soothingly, still wondering how to introduce the feathers without sounding foolish. "Um, I keep finding feathers on my bed," I said finally.

"Must be a leak in your goose-down pillow. I'll take a look—"

"No, no, I'm sure these aren't goose feathers. One was green and one black."

Delia frowned at me, then her face relaxed. "There's a fireplace in your room. Must be birds getting in there. Jed'll have to climb to the roof and stop up that chimney."

That must be the answer, I told myself with relief, ashamed I hadn't thought of it.

"You know," Delia said, "your asking about me locking up at night reminds me that Miss Faith got to asking me that very same question most every morning in the last couple months before she died. 'Delia,' she'd say, 'are you sure?' So we'd try the doors together and every time we'd find 'em locked tight. Just before she passed on, she mentioned having Jed put bolts on the inside."

"I notice he didn't do it."

Delia shrugged. "After Miss Faith died I didn't see any reason for bolts. Naranada ain't exactly what they call a high-crime area."

"Do you think my great-aunt believed an intruder was getting into the house at night?"

"You got to remember her mind sort of wandered there toward the end. Weren't no reason to think there was robbers about when I never found anything out of place nor missing."

I went out to watch Tibbie ride and when we came back to the house later, the phone rang as we entered the kitchen.

"It's for you, Miss Valora," Lucy called from the entry. My great-aunt had regarded telephones as undesirable necessities, and the only one she'd had in the house was in an alcove off the entry.

I picked up the phone and gave my name.

"This is Luis." His voice sent a prickle of awareness along my nerves. "I'm calling to ask how Tibbie's injured foot is faring."

"She's right here," I said hastily, not certain I
wanted to talk to him. "I'll let her tell you herself." I
handed Tibbie the phone, saying, "It's Dr. Redhawk."

"Hi," Tibbie said. "My foot doesn't hurt at all. I
can even run okay. I'm learning to ride Misty, too. Jed
says I'm getting to be pretty fair on horseback and
maybe someday I'll make a real rider." She listened for
a moment, then said, "Sure, that'd be neat. She likes
picnics, too."

Before I could ask any questions, Tibbie said goodbye and hung up. "We're going on a picnic with Dr.
Redhawk," she told me excitedly. "And I'll get to
meet Running Fox."

It took me a few seconds to recall that Running Fox
was Luis's shaman grandfather. "You might have
asked me if I wanted to go on a picnic," I said.

Tibbie raised her eyebrows. "Why wouldn't you?
You told me yourself that picnics are the most interesting, if exasperating, way to eat ever experienced by
man or woman."

My daughter's memory was very efficient, especially when it was to her advantage. "Just when is this
picnic?" I asked.

"This afternoon, 'cause Dr. Redhawk takes
Wednesday afternoons off. I never met a real Indian
medicine man before—did you?"

I shook my head, aware that it wasn't so much that
I didn't want to go but that I didn't think it wise to be
in Luis's company more than necessary. Still, I hated

to disappoint Tibbie and, after all, I wouldn't be alone with him.

"It sounds like fun," I told her.

By the time Luis came by to pick us up in his battered four-wheel drive, I'd made up my mind to let nothing disturb my resolution to be no more than casually friendly. Since he focused his attention on Tibbie, at first I had no trouble keeping my resolve.

"Can I ask you a question about your grandfather?" she said to him as we bounced over a road that was little more than a dirt track into the foothills.

He smiled at her. "Ask away."

"Do I say Mr. Running Fox or just Mr. Fox?"

"I think he'd like it best if you called him 'Grandfather' because that's the name the Miwok children use."

"Even though they're not related to him?"

"Right."

Tibbie thought this over. "Okay," she said finally. "Actually, I don't really have any grandfathers."

"I'm happy to share mine with you."

"Is he very scary?"

Luis glanced reassuringly at Tibbie. "I can guarantee he won't do anything to scare you. He'll probably tell you—and whatever other kids happen to be around—Miwok stories. Passing on stories of our people is part of a medicine man's work."

Listening to the two of them, I wondered if Luis's interest in Tibbie was more than casual. The same question had crossed my mind when I'd observed Travis's patience with my daughter when we swam in his pool. Did one or the other of them have a hidden reason for befriending Tibbie? Because surely the man who'd fathered her must know she was his child.

I thrust the notion from my mind. Jack Norton, I told myself firmly, was also a possibility, no matter what Willa had said.

When we stopped near a scattering of huts and old trailers among valley live oaks, I was glad to leave the heat of Luis's car for the shade of the trees.

Dogs and several toddlers, naked from the waist down, escorted us as Luis, carrying a basket, led the way toward one of the oaks near a small stream. Underneath the tree sat a man whose braided dark hair was barely tinged with gray, though it was obvious from the many creases in his face that he was far from young.

"My grandfather," Luis said to him, "I bring guests. This is Valora Rolland and her daughter, Tibbie."

Running Fox's penetrating dark gaze met mine, probing for and finding, I felt, my each and every secret. It wasn't until his eyes shifted to Tibbie that I managed to greet him.

"Hello, Grandfather," she said, and he smiled at her.

"You're welcome here," he told us. "I enjoy meeting people, but this grandson of mine doesn't often bring guests."

The dogs and the toddlers, losing interest, wandered off toward the stream, the water too low to pose a danger even to the smallest. Then an older child, a girl about Tibbie's age, poked her head from behind the trunk of the oak to stare at us.

"Come and join us, Soso," Running Fox said without looking around. "You haven't heard all of the story. I will begin again for Tibbie."

Shyly the girl edged from behind the tree trunk and came to sit beside the old man. Hesitantly, with sidelong looks at me, Tibbie eased to the ground on his other side. The two girls examined each other with interest.

"This is a story of how the world came to be," Running Fox began. "Listen well, for what I say is true. Before the People were created, there were six different races in the world...."

Luis touched my arm and gestured away from his grandfather toward another oak. He made signs indicating we could sit on its broad lower limb. Since it was near enough to keep Tibbie in sight, I nodded.

He set the basket at the base of his grandfather's oak and then we walked to the other tree. Before I could attempt to scramble onto the branch, he grasped me by the waist, lifted me there and then pulled himself up to sit next to me.

Running Fox's singsong chant, as he told the story to the girls, was low enough so I could make out only an occasional phrase. His words mingled with the faint gurgle of the stream and the muted twitter of birds in the oaks, and this soothing background murmur, combined with the heat of the day, made me drowsy. Without warning, I yawned, not covering my mouth quickly enough to escape Luis's gaze.

He raised an eyebrow. "I can't believe *I* caused that. Haven't you been sleeping well?"

I shrugged, a bit miffed at his arrogance, true though it might be that I couldn't imagine ever being bored by Luis. "Bad dreams," I muttered.

"Want to share them?"

"It's nothing, really. I've dreamed twice that my great-aunt is warning me, though I'm not sure what of. Each time she's handed me a feather."

We were sitting close enough so I felt rather than saw him stiffen. "What kind of a feather?"

I hadn't a clue why the mention of feathers had put him on alert, but I saw no reason not to answer his question. "First a hummingbird's green feather, then one from a red-winged blackbird."

"In your dreams, did your great-aunt say anything about the feathers?"

I frowned, surprised at his interest. "Something about bloodred and the blackbird carrying death. You know how dreams are. Ominous at the time but when you wake they don't make any sense. I'm sure the feathers must have been left by birds coming down the chimney into the fireplace in my bedroom."

"The feathers were real, then?" His voice, low until now, rose.

"I found them on my bed," I admitted, taken aback by his intensity.

He shook his head. "I told you coming back to Naranada was a mistake. Now your great-aunt is also warning you."

"But she's dead!"

"Her spirit lives."

I stared at him, unable to believe my ears. "Her ghost, you mean? Come on, Luis!"

He shifted, straddling the limb so he faced me. "Have you forgotten so easily, Valora? Have you dismissed what was released that night as only something you imagined?"

I quivered inwardly, aware he meant the night on Mount Sangre. "How could I forget? I was scared out of my wits. But afterward I realized it could have been the storm. It must have been the storm."

He reached a hand toward me as though to grip my arm but drew it back before touching me. "Rationalization is dangerous. Neither you nor Tibbie should be within a hundred miles of Mount Sangre."

I did my best to remain calm despite my growing irritation with his new attempt at inducing me to leave Naranada. "Luis, you're a doctor. You must know better than to believe in ghosts and—"

"Yes, I'm a doctor, but I'm also one of the People, and I learned young not to depend entirely on what I could see with my eyes and hear with my ears." He released me. "Some things can only be sensed by the spirit. Don't close yourself off from your dream warnings. Dreams often carry the truth in symbolic imagery."

My attempt to smile at his words failed, but I was far from convinced. "I suppose I'd have to agree with you about dreams in the Freudian sense, but I'm too old and too practical to start believing in spirit warnings."

He was silent for a time. "Would you listen to my grandfather?" he said at last.

I blinked. "What does he have to do with this?"

"He knows what happened ten years ago. When he finishes his story, I want you to tell him everything you can remember about your dreams. I'll amuse the girls while you do."

As I thought about what he'd said, I listened absently to Running Fox's words. "No one knows who the fifth race of people were nor what happened to them. Perhaps the wind blew them away. Threw them away. But they must have been evil. Why else would they have vanished without a trace?''

Evil. It was difficult for me to accept that pure evil existed when even the most vicious of serial killers always seemed to have twisted childhoods to explain their terrible crimes.

As the shaman finished his tale, Luis lifted me down from the oak branch, holding me against him longer than necessary but not as long as I wanted him to. I knew better than to risk involvement with him so why did I have no willpower where he was concerned?

After Luis suggested to Tibbie and Soso that the three of them wade in the creek, I was left alone with Running Fox.

"Your spirit looks upon darkness," the old man said, his perception unnerving me. "Sit here beside me and we will talk."

"I've had disturbing dreams," I admitted as I sank down next to him. Luis had insisted I tell him about the feathers and so I did.

A silence fell when I finished. Glancing at him, I saw that his eyes were closed. "Nothing good ever comes from dream gifts," he said, "but it's too late to tell you not to take anything offered in a dream—you've already taken the two feathers. There will be four feathers. You've been given hummingbird and blackbird. Two more will come to you. Until I know what birds those feathers belong to, the meaning is hidden."

Opening his eyes, he reached for my hand, holding it between his. "Darkness travels with you, the same darkness that touches my grandson and clouds the path of the child you've taken for your daughter."

Tibbie! I caught my breath.

"When you bring me all four of the feathers," he went on, "I will know what to do. Your people so easily say, 'Take care,' and the words mean nothing. Listen, for my words have meaning. Watch over your daughter. She holds a a secret hidden from her and so from me, as well. Keep her from the place of evil."

I moistened my dry lips with my tongue before I could speak. "Do you mean Mount Sangre?"

"My people call it Hamaua's home. Hamaua is a dark and dangerous spirit. Keep away—you and your daughter." He released my hand and I rose.

Running Fox sprang up with the agility of a much younger man. Though slightly shrunken with age, he was still tall, like his grandson. He wore an ordinary blue denim shirt and jeans, but I decided nothing could ever make him look ordinary. Strangely, I felt he did have the power he claimed, the power to help me if I needed help. I hoped I never would.

Unexpectedly he smiled at me. "Luis has chosen well," he said.

His meaning was clear enough. Flustered, I could only blink at him. He must be wrong. All Luis seemed to want was for me to take Tibbie and leave Naranada forever.

Before we left the Miwok settlement, Running Fox called Luis to him and they spoke together while I talked to Tibbie and Soso.

"Soso says she comes into Naranada sometimes and I invited her to Bloodstone House to ride Misty," Tibbie told me. "We can take turns."

"That's great. Do you ride?" I asked Soso.

She nodded, shy with me as she hadn't been with Tibbie or Luis. "I hope you can visit soon," I told Soso. "Tibbie and I will look forward to seeing you."

"I'll come." Soso's voice was soft and low, blending into the murmur of the stream. "Tibbie and me, we're friends."

Tibbie beamed at her in obvious agreement. "Did you know Soso's name means *squirrel?*" she asked me. "The kind in trees, not the ones that live in the ground. I wish my name meant something."

"Actually it does," I assured her. "Tabitha means gazelle—that's an animal something like an antelope."

"Or a deer?" Tibbie asked.

I stretched the definition to please her. "You could say so."

"You're a squirrel and I'm a deer," Tibbie told Soso, and they giggled in unison. When the fit of giggles ended, Tibbie said to me, "Luis invited Soso to come along on our picnic."

I raised my eyebrows. "Luis? What happened to 'Dr. Redhawk'?"

"He told me I could call him 'Luis' like Soso does. Okay?" After my nod, she added, "We're leaving the basket for Grandfather. Our picnic stuff is in Luis's cooler and he's taking us to a secret place."

Luis joined us, leading the way to his four-wheel drive. The two girls scrambled into the back, and once again we jolted over an all but invisible road that ended at a pile of huge granite boulders.

"Please wait in the car with the girls until I return," Luis said as he opened his door. He slid out and I thought I heard him begin chanting as he eased through a narrow space between two of the boulders before disappearing from sight.

"Why is Luis leaving us here?" Tibbie asked.

I was about to tell her I had no idea, when Soso spoke. "'Cause of the snakes. He has to tell them to go away and not bother us."

"Snakes!" I cried, peering over the seat at her. "What snakes?"

Soso shrugged. "Just snakes. In case they're there. Grandfather taught Luis the right words."

Though I'd never seen one in my life, belatedly I recalled that rattlesnakes supposedly flourished in the back country. I certainly wanted no part of rattlers.

When Luis came back to the car I told him so.

"There aren't any snakes, rattlers or otherwise, where we're going," he assured me, reaching into the back for the cooler.

I eyed him dubiously.

"Don't you trust me?" he asked.

"*I* trust you," Tibbie announced, climbing out. Soso followed her. Reluctantly I left the safety of the car, glancing nervously at the ground.

Luis hefted the cooler. "This way," he said.

"Luis," I said. "Are you sure—?"

He shot me an irate glance. "Do you really think I'd lead you and the girls into danger, Valora?"

I shook my head, finding I couldn't believe he would.

"Then let's go," he said.

We followed Luis through the cleft between boulders twice as high as my head. Once through the narrow space, I stopped short, drawing in my breath in pleased surprise. We stood in a rock-ringed oasis. Water gurgled up from the ground, forming a small pool before trickling through an opening between the stones. A sycamore, the girth of its white trunk betraying its vast age, shaded the pool while small green shrubs and grass edged the water.

"This is a really, truly secret place," Tibbie said happily.

"It's a good place," Soso agreed. She fixed her gaze on Luis. "A sacred place?"

"Only in the sense that bad things won't happen here," he told her.

She nodded, satisfied. I wasn't. Though I felt the peacefulness surrounding me, I doubted anyone could ever be certain where or when bad things might happen.

"So when do we eat?" Tibbie asked.

The food was ordinary enough—sandwiches of peanut butter and of cheese, served with soft drinks—but eating in the secret world shut away among the boulders seemed to add a special flavor. When they'd eaten their fill, Soso and Tibbie sat side by side at the edge of the pool, dangling their bare feet in the water and talking animatedly.

Luis and I weren't as friendly. In his jeans and T-shirt, he leaned against one of the giant boulders, seeming to stare into the branches of the sycamore, but I knew he saw nothing but his own thoughts.

"You used to wear jeans when you worked in Great-aunt Faith's garden," I told him finally. "And the same brooding expression."

He turned his head to gaze at me. "Not if you were around."

"Actually, I used to spy on you a lot from the windows," I admitted. "My great-aunt always made such an awful fuss if she saw me talking to you."

"I know." His voice was dark and terse, making me realize I hadn't been the only one she'd chided.

"She was old-fashioned," I said.

"She was prejudiced." He spoke flatly, without rancor. "I didn't think you were, but you were so elusive I could never be sure."

I tried to explain how I'd felt then. "You unsettled me."

"You did a hell of a lot more than that to me." He pushed away from the boulder and crossed to where I sat in the shade with my back propped against one of the giant rocks. He eased down beside me.

Though we weren't touching, it suddenly felt as though every cell in my body became acutely aware of Luis's nearness.

"If it hadn't been for that night on Mount Sangre—" He paused, sighing. "I knew at the time I should have stopped Travis."

"I'm not certain you could have. He was so determined to—"

"I should have knocked the son of a bitch flat, taken that damned book away from him and burned it."

I blinked at the venom in his voice. "My great-aunt did burn it," I told him.

"Too late."

"If we're getting into blaming, it wasn't all Travis's fault," I said. "I never should have let him take the book from our library in the first place."

"Did she ever find the medallion?" Luis asked.

I stared at him, wondering how he knew Great-aunt Faith had been looking for it.

Evidently reading my thoughts, he said impatiently, "I was her doctor the last few years of her life and she confided in me as much as she did anyone. Which wasn't a hell of a lot."

"Delia thinks my great-aunt forgot where she'd put whatever she was looking for," I told him.

"The medallion," he insisted.

I shrugged, knowing he was right.

"God grant it's never found." His words were fervent. He leaned his head back and closed his eyes. "I came here to relax, not to call up the past. Sorry."

He didn't speak again or open his eyes. I tried shutting my eyes, too, in the hope the peace of the oasis might soak into me, but it was too late to exclude the past.

Behind my closed lids I could once again see myself and Travis ten years ago, sorting books in the Rolland library, see myself finding the thin and battered old volume tucked away behind other books on the highest shelf, glancing at the strange words on the crumbling pages before handing it to Travis, asking what he made of the book.

He'd leafed through it, frowning at first, then becoming excited. "I'd say we've found a *grimoire!* You know—a book of spells."

I hadn't the slightest idea what he'd meant at the time and when I did learn that danger hid among those moldering pages, it was too late. Much too late.

CHAPTER FIVE

Even with my eyes closed I could sense Luis beside me as we both leaned back against one of the boulders forming the hidden sanctuary. He remained silent. The only sounds were the subdued voices of the two girls and the quiet murmur of the water. Still my mind was anything but peaceful as I tried in vain to stop my morbid exhumation of the past....

After I'd given Travis the strange, old, hand-bound volume from the Rolland library, he'd found a tarnished silver medallion tucked inside an inner flap. An enameled white owl in flight with talons extended was etched into the metal and strange symbols circled the bird. I didn't like the look of the thing, but Travis handled it with reverence.

"Hey, this is fantastic," Travis said. "Unbelievable! I'd really like to study the book and see if I can discover the meaning of these letters on the medallion. I doubt if anyone's looked at the book in years, so it shouldn't make any difference if I take both of them home for a couple of days."

I glanced dubiously at Travis. Great-aunt Faith wasn't a lender of anything. Still, she might not even know the book was in the library, tucked away as it had been behind others. Travis wasn't asking much—I'd never seen him so excited as he was over this moldy old volume—and I hated to refuse his request. If I went to ask my great-aunt's permission for him to borrow the book, it would be the same as me saying no here and now.

"Aw, come on, Val, she'll never miss it," he coaxed, as if aware of her reputation for possessiveness. "I promise I'll return it *muy pronto.*"

"Well, I guess maybe it's all right."

"I knew I could count on you!" He flung an arm around my waist, caught me to him and kissed me quickly. "Sorry to desert you," he said as he let me go, "but I'm kind of in a hurry this morning."

In a hurry to get out of the house with the book before my great-aunt discovered he had it, I told myself, half my mind occupied with why Travis's kiss, though pleasant enough, didn't send bubbles dancing through me the way even a sidelong glance from Luis could.

Travis phoned the next morning. "I've got a great idea for your birthday," he said.

"You know Great-aunt Faith is giving a birthday party for me this afternoon," I reminded him.

"Yeah, yeah, but this'll be later. At night. And there needs to be four of us—two girls and two guys."

Confused, I asked, "A double date, you mean?"

"Not exactly. You get the girl, I'll get the guy, okay?"

"Corenna's at Avila Beach with her folks for the rest of the month and I don't really know any of the other girls in town well enough to—"

"What about Willa?"

"I'm not sure she'd want to."

Travis snorted. "She'll be flattered out of her tiny mind and you know it."

Since he was right about Willa being flattered, I said only, "Don't be snide—she's as smart as you are."

He laughed. "I resent that. *No one's* as smart as T. J. York. So you ask her, okay?"

"First tell me what we're going to do."

"Can't, it's a secret. But I swear you'll never have another birthday present even remotely like this one. Be a sweetheart and don't argue, just ask Willa. And *don't* tell your great-aunt."

"But if I'm going out at night I'll have to tell her."

"Not if you sneak out. Look, I'll clue you in this afternoon at your great-aunt's tea or whatever the hell she's going to serve."

He hung up and I was left puzzled and a touch uneasy, not at all sure I wanted to be a part of Travis's secret. Still, since he was doing it for me, I ought to cooperate just as I was cooperating with Great-aunt Faith in her notion of a party.

My great-aunt had invited Travis and the Wilson twins, Jenny and Penny, for ice cream and cake in the morning room from two to four. The twins were her idea of the type of girl I should associate with—but not mine. Nor did Jenny and Penny particularly care for me, though they all but swooned over Travis. He passed the two hours flirting with them, walked them gallantly to the door when the hall clock struck four, then returned to grab my hand and urge me through the French doors and into the rose garden.

"I was bored out of my gourd," he moaned. "How do you stand them?"

"I don't see much of Jenny and Penny." I spoke absently, having caught sight of Luis cutting the hedge beyond the garden. He would have enlivened the party considerably, at least as far as I was concerned, but I'd known better than to suggest to my great-aunt that he be invited.

Travis noticed him, too. "Luis!" he called, motioning him over.

As Luis sauntered up I tried not to, as Corenna would have put it, melt. As a result I stood stiff and proper in my very conservative pink cotton, a gift from my great-aunt.

"Can you join us tonight?" Travis asked Luis, to my surprise. The two of them didn't pal around together at all.

"Depends," Luis said.

He hadn't yet looked at me, not that I'd seen anyway.

"Val's coming and Willa," Travis said. "It's sort of an impromptu celebration for Val's birthday. At midnight."

My eyes widened. Midnight!

Luis glanced at me and I swallowed. "Where?" he asked.

Having no idea, I shook my head.

"We'll meet here near the barn at eleven-thirty," Travis said, smiling smugly, "and then I'll reveal all."

I might have protested if Luis hadn't said, "I'll be there."

I hardly ever got to talk to Luis, with my great-aunt on the alert to be certain I didn't bother the "help" while they were working. If Luis were coming, then I was, too.

Later, I cornered Willa in the upstairs hall and brought her into my room. "I know it's scant notice," I said, "but I'm inviting you to a party tonight that Travis is giving for me."

Willa blinked. "Oh, damn," she muttered, then flushed as though fearing I might scold her for the "damn" as my great-aunt would have. She leaned closer and lowered her voice. "I told Jack I'd meet him tonight."

"In that case—"

"No, wait. I'll call and cancel it. He won't be too upset—he knows I have trouble getting away from the house."

"Look, Willa, it's not necessary to—"

"I'd *rather* go to your party," she insisted.

"I'm not too sure what Travis has planned," I warned.

"I don't care. I'm sure it'll be fun. Oh, I'm so excited!"

"Maybe you'll change your mind when I tell you we have to sneak out and meet him at the barn a half hour before midnight."

Willa shrugged. "No big deal. I was going to have to sneak out anyway." She caressed the cat's-eye ring I'd given her. "Thanks a million for asking me."

Luis and Travis were waiting by the barn when Willa and I arrived. The full moon rode high so none of us had bothered with flashlights. In my opinion the silvery light lent a romantic flavor to the night, enhancing Luis's dark good looks and turning Travis into a quasi-Apollo.

"Moonlight steals all the color and makes everything strange," Willa said as we came up to the guys. "It's almost like we're in a different, unfriendly land."

Her words took me aback. I'd never thought of moonlight as unfriendly.

As Travis greeted Willa, Luis slipped something small and paper wrapped into my hand. It felt like a thin book.

"Happy birthday, Valora." His voice was so low I scarcely heard him.

Thrilled but flustered—Luis had never given me anything before—I murmured my thanks before giving in to my impulse to hide his gift from the others. Planning to retrieve it later, I slipped Luis's gift into the wooden box Jed had attached to the barn door to hold his pipe, tobacco pouch and matches when he was working.

"What now?" Luis asked Travis.

"Onward and upward," Travis said, picking up a black bag, grasping my hand and pulling me with him as he strode away from the barn.

Luis, with Willa in tow, caught up immediately. "Onward and upward where?" he demanded.

"To the top of the mountain, where else?"

"Mount Sangre?" Luis asked.

"You got it."

"That's not the greatest place to—"

Travis cut him off. "It's the only place. Once we get started you'll understand what I mean."

Luis subsided but his disapproval showed in his scowl.

"I've never been to a midnight party before." Willa's voice was breathless.

Travis shot her a smile. "I guarantee this is one party you'll never forget."

I'd climbed Mount Sangre several times but never at night. All at once it seemed daring and adventurous to be struggling up the steep hill while clouds alternately concealed and revealed the moon. While I hadn't agreed with Willa's description of moonlight, I now decided night itself changed the world, darkness making everything mysteriously unlike what we saw by day. Different and more exciting.

Knowing my great-aunt would have a fit if she knew what I was doing added a fillip to our midnight escapade.

Below us, the ordinary night sounds of the country and of the nearby town were muted—even the usually loud roar of a motorcycle seemed to come from another, far-off world.

Willa giggled nervously. "I wonder if that's Jack," she whispered to me. "I don't think he believed what I told him."

We climbed so quickly that by the time we reached the top I was out of breath and would have paused to rest if Travis hadn't herded us all over to a large and rounded stone with a flattened top several feet above the ground and about five feet in diameter. I remembered the rock from my other climbs and also recalled the rumor that the visible part of the stone was but the top of an immense rock that thrust deep into the ground.

When we reached the rock, Luis said, "This isn't a good place. Let's move farther away."

Travis ignored him, setting the black bag on the stone and opening it. The three of us watched as, in the shimmering moonlight, he removed a thick black candle, lit it, let wax drip onto the rock and then stuck the base of the candle into the congealing wax so it stood steady. I expected the flame to wink out but the night was still, with no wind, and, although the flame flicked unevenly, the candle remained lit.

"Left over from my folks' Halloween party," he said. "Otherwise I might have had trouble locating a black candle on short notice."

None of us asked why the candle had to be black. I didn't because my sense of adventure was rapidly fading and I wasn't too sure I liked being there. Perhaps it was the effect of the candlelight on Travis's face, creating shadows that changed him to a stranger. Or maybe it was Luis's dark scowl. Or the tense grip of Willa's fingers as she linked her hand with mine. In any case, I found I didn't want to know why the candle must be black.

"Val," Travis said, "I want you to stand to the east." He pointed and I shrugged, disentangled my fingers from Willa's and moved where he told me. He ordered Willa to the west and Luis to the south, while he remained north of the stone.

"North is the position of power," he explained.

"You don't want to use power up here," Luis muttered.

"What's the matter, Redhawk, you scared?" Travis challenged.

Luis bristled. "Not me. But the girls—"

"You're not afraid, are you, Willa?" Travis demanded.

"N-no." Her voice belied her disclaimer.

"And Val isn't afraid of anything," Travis insisted, not giving me a chance to speak. "So here we go. Don't say anything, just watch and listen."

He lifted a small bottle from the bag, twisted off the cap and poured a clotted reddish substance onto the stone, forming a circle. I wrinkled my nose against the sweetish, vaguely unpleasant odor, wondering what in heaven's name he was up to. When he placed the owl medallion carefully into the center of the circle, I frowned. Next he removed the battered book I'd let him borrow and that was too much for me.

"Travis," I began, "I—"

"I told you to be quiet!" he snapped. "Tell me later."

Subsiding, I glared at him while he opened the book. Holding it in his hands but not looking at the pages, he began to intone strange names:

"Eloah Va-Daath, Elohim Gibor, Elohim Tzabaoth, Ehieh, Iod, El, Tetragrammaton Elohim, El Adonai Tzabaoth, Shaddai. Ye great and all-powerful Nine, I, Travis Jonathan York, by the sacrifice of blood and by virtue of the sacred owl, call ye forth. I command that ye come to me and do my bidding."

I tried to find what he was doing amusing so I could laugh and dispel the chill settling over me despite the warm night, but there was nothing funny in his intensity or in the eerie and strangely malevolent words he uttered. As though caught in a web woven by those words, I neither moved nor spoke while Travis repeated the invocation two more times.

Luis and Willa were also silent. When Travis finished, somewhere in the stillness of the night I heard the sinister hooting of an owl. Without intending to, I counted the hoots. Seven. *The magic number.* The recollection came to me from childhood tales. But there was nothing childish about what Travis had done.

A single white feather spun down from darkness above the stone onto the medallion, its tip touching and stained by the red circle. I gasped, suddenly understanding the circle was of blood. Though sickened, I found myself unable to look away.

A golden flash from across the stone where Willa stood with her arms upraised broke my trance. I looked uncomprehendingly at her, not at first connecting the golden glow with the cat's-eye ring she wore.

My unease turned to stark fear as the candle winked out, the glow faded and we were left in total darkness with no moon, no stars and no familiar town lights below. Willa screamed. Luis cursed. Travis laughed, an eerie, triumphant sound that raised the hair on my nape.

A bolt of brilliant light sizzled down, striking the rock, then a ferocious blast flung me backward, stunning me. Rain sluiced down, soaking me as I sprawled helpless on my back, terror stricken, unable to move or speak. A sense of wrongness hovered in the darkness, a horror I couldn't begin to identify.

Finally the rain splashing onto my face brought back enough of my wits so I managed to struggle to my feet.

I could see no one in the darkness. Opening my mouth to call to Luis, I hesitated. Though I knew I had to be on Mount Sangre, I felt that I was, instead, in a strange, malevolent place with danger seeking me. If I spoke, I was doomed. I knew I must flee. But where? In what direction? Blackness surrounded me; I had no clue where safety might lie.

Swallowing my pleas for help, I reached out with my foot, feeling cautiously for the hardness of the stone. When I finally touched hard rock, I turned my back to it and edged away, trying to move carefully and quietly. Terror overrode all other impulses and I started to run blindly in a pell-mell flight downhill, stumbling, falling, pushing myself to my feet and running again until I crashed into the old shed at the bottom, banging my head so hard I was forced to lean dizzily against the shed for support.

Drenched, gasping with pain and fear, I groped along the rough wood until I found the gaping maw of the doorless opening and eased inside, out of the rain. Though the roof leaked in places, it was a relief to be protected from the relentless downpour and I was able to recover enough to think more clearly.

The mindless terror I'd felt on Mount Sangre had diminished to simple fright. The darkness of the storm made me uneasy but I no longer believed unknown and hideous danger lurked nearby. If anyone had been in the shed when I entered he'd have either attacked me by now or made himself known, so I believed I was alone. I regained enough of my courage to call into the night, "Luis! Willa! Travis!"

I thought I heard a distant cry. My name? Unsure, I shouted again and again. I'd almost given up when I heard Luis's voice close by.

"Valora, where are you?"

"In the shed."

He stumbled through the opening and I clutched him thankfully. He wrapped his arms around me and, both drenched to the skin, we held each other wordlessly. The warmth of his body and the strength of his arms comforted me, making me feel I was safe. Luis would protect me; he wouldn't let anything bad happen.

At last I said, "Where are the others?"

"You're the first one I've found," he said, easing his hold but not letting me go completely.

I snuggled against him, reluctant to lose my safe haven. "Up there," I whispered, "it was awful."

"I shouldn't have let him go on," Luis muttered.

I stiffened as a dreadful thought came to mind. "You don't suppose lightning hit Willa or Travis, do you?"

"That wasn't lightning."

I pulled away, staring up at him even though I couldn't see his face in the darkness. "It must have been. Right after that it started to rain."

"Something that was bound into the rock broke loose."

"What on earth are you talking about?" I demanded.

"My grandfather told me about the evil on Mount Sangre," Luis said. "Travis set that evil free."

I couldn't accept what he said. Travis, I felt sure, had memorized a spell from the old book I should never have let him borrow and had gone through a lot of scary mumbo jumbo before the storm began—but freeing evil? I shook my head and was about to argue with Luis when I heard Travis calling me.

I turned to the doorway, shouting Travis's name. "We're in the shed," I cried.

Moments later Travis stumbled inside.

"Where's Willa?" I demanded, guilt mingling with fear for her. If I hadn't invited her, poor Willa would have gone with Jack and wouldn't be wherever she was now.

"I don't know where Willa is," Travis said.

"We've got to find her immediately!" I cried and plunged from the shed just as the moon broke through the thinning clouds.

The rain had diminished to sprinkles and, by the moon's intermittent light, we searched for Willa, calling her name over and over without any response.

"She's probably found her way back to your house by now," Travis said after a while.

I wanted to believe him, to go home and find Willa there waiting for me—but what if she wasn't? "We'd better climb the hill and look first," I said with great reluctance. I never wanted to go up Mount Sangre again.

But we did, the three of us, and the closer we came to the summit, the more apprehensive I grew. I might not believe in Luis's Miwok evil, but I was so terrified that when I tried to call Willa's name no sound came from my paralyzed throat. As we arrived at the top, clouds covered the moon. All was blackness. When I reached to either side to clutch Luis and Travis, I found only empty space. It was as though they'd been swallowed up by the earth.

Unable to utter a sound, I stumbled ahead, arms flailing in a desperate search for either of them, and fell headlong over an obstacle. As I tried frantically to scramble to my feet, I felt hair under my hands, then skin. My trembling fingers traced the outline of a nose, a mouth, an ear. When I touched the tiny rounded earring in the earlobe, I realized what I'd fallen over. Willa's body.

The moon sailed free of the clouds and I saw to my confusion that she was completely naked. Certain she was dead, my heart pounded in dread as I reached for her hand. She was lying not far from the rock, as though she'd been flung there by the blast and never moved afterward. The blast, though, couldn't have stripped off her clothes.

When I grasped her hand, to my great relief, she moaned. Luis and Travis rushed up and Luis gathered her scattered clothes. Wet as they were, I covered her with them, not wanting to leave her exposed. But no matter how I coaxed her to respond, she remained unconscious and it became clear that Luis and Travis would have to carry her home.

With their help, I managed to slip Willa's dress over her head and onto her body before they lifted her from the ground. Thank God my great-aunt had grown somewhat hard-of-hearing or else we'd have had her to face when we came dragging in with Willa. As it was, Delia heard and came down, confronting us in the kitchen while we were debating about calling a doctor.

"What's all this?" Delia demanded, hands on her hips. Taking one look at Willa, she didn't wait for an answer. "You boys carry her straight up to her room— I'll show you the way."

Once Willa was on her bed, Delia started to shoo Luis and Travis from the house, but I stopped her. "Give me back that book and what came with it," I demanded of Travis.

He hesitated, then pulled the book from the inside of his shirt. "The medallion's not here," he said. "I lost it along with the bag."

I set the very damp volume on the kitchen table and said, "The medallion belongs to Great-aunt Faith. You'd better find it."

"I'll look for it tomorrow," he assured me.

More concerned with Willa than anything else, still I noticed that Travis seemed dazed, unlike Luis. Or myself, for that matter. I was upset and frightened but not dazed.

"I'll have a look at Willa," Delia said to me. "You go down with the boys and lock up after they're gone. Then take off those wet clothes."

Relieved to turn the responsibility over to someone older and wiser, I saw Luis and Travis out, hurried to my room, stripped, flung on a bathrobe and returned to Willa's room. Delia had taken off Willa's wet dress and Willa was once again moaning.

"What do you think's the matter with her?" I asked apprehensively.

Delia fixed me with a stern eye. "You should know better'n me."

I gave her an extremely edited account of what had happened, finishing with, "I think Willa might have been struck by lightning."

"Never heard that lightning took off a body's underclothes and still left a dress on them."

I bit my lip. Finding Willa naked had been one of the things I hadn't mentioned.

"No," Willa moaned. "No, no, no."

"It's all right, dearie," Delia murmured. "You're safe and sound in your own bed." To me she said, "Fetch me one of her nightgowns."

Together, we got Willa into the gown. She didn't fight us but she didn't cooperate, either, not exactly unconscious but seemingly unaware of where she was.

I was on the verge of asking Delia if she thought we ought to call a doctor when Willa's eyes opened and focused on me. "Valora," she whispered.

I sat on the bed and leaned over her. "How do you feel?" I asked.

"Sore all over." Her voice was stronger. Spotting Delia, she blinked. "Have I been sick?" she asked.

Confused, I replied, "Don't you remember going with me earlier tonight?"

"Sort of but not exactly. What did we do?"

"You don't remember climbing Mount Sangre?"

"No. Did we?"

I questioned her until Delia made me stop, saying Willa needed to rest.

"I'll help you wash up and then give you an aspirin with some warm milk to help you sleep," she told Willa. "As for you, missy, into bed with you this minute. I don't doubt Miss Faith will have something to say about all this in the morning."

From the first I'd realized Delia would tell my great-aunt. At least I'd have a few hours' respite before I had to face her.

I fell into bed exhausted, but every time I began to drift into sleep, I jerked awake in panic, staring fearfully into the darkness of my room. Finally I left my bedside lamp on and dozed off, only to enter a nightmare world where I was pursued by nameless monsters. I woke in the late morning with my heart pounding, hardly able to believe I was actually in my own room. And safe.

I slipped from my bed and tiptoed to Willa's room. She was asleep. Unlike mine, her sleep seemed to be peaceful. Not at all eager to face Great-aunt Faith, I dressed and crept down the back stairs to the kitchen and Delia.

"So you're up," Delia said when she saw me.

"I didn't sleep very well."

"Lies make poor bedfellows," Delia said, putting her hands on her hips. "When I helped Willa get into the bathtub and wash before I left her, it came clear to me what happened to her last night."

I stared at her. "I don't understand."

Delia's eyes narrowed. "She'd been interfered with, that's what. And don't tell me you didn't know."

It took me a moment or two to decipher Delia's meaning. "You mean Willa was—raped?"

"That's a word I don't care to use but, yes, she was, and no mistake."

My horrified expression must have convinced her I'd truly not known, because her face softened a trifle. "Willa, now, she don't remember a thing about it. If you're telling the truth about having to look for her, I suppose the filthy beast who attacked her might have come on her when she was alone."

"Oh, my God," I whispered, slumping into a chair and putting my hand over my eyes, Delia's words ringing in my ears.

Filthy beast. Delia was right. Any man who'd do such a rotten thing was a beast.

"But no one was with us except Travis and Luis," I blurted, looking up at Delia.

Delia shrugged. "According to what you told me, either of them could've done it. You said yourself you were alone in the shed for a while."

Luis? Travis? I couldn't believe it! And then I recalled hearing a motorcycle when we were on Mount Sangre.

"Jack Norton!" I cried. "It might have been Jack. Willa broke a date with him to go with me and he could have been mad about that and followed us." The more I thought about Jack being the guilty one, the better I liked the explanation.

"Could've been." Delia spoke flatly. "If he did follow you. But there ain't no ruling out the other two—there's three possibilities. Unless some stranger wandered by in the storm, which I doubt."

"Maybe Willa will remember," I said hopefully.

"Miss Faith's waiting for you in the morning room," Delia told me. "She said you could have breakfast first."

I shook my head, knowing I'd never be able to force down a single bite, took a deep breath and walked slowly to the morning room where I found my great-aunt seated at the glass-topped table. I'd never seen her look so grim.

"Sit down, Valora," she ordered.

I obeyed.

"Delia has told me the entire shameful story," she said sharply. "I'm deeply disappointed in you. Deeply disappointed."

Having no words to defend myself, I didn't try.

"You'll be leaving for home tomorrow," she said. "I've arranged for your transportation to the Visalia airport, your flight to Arizona and have notified your mother and your stepfather to expect you. It will be up to you to explain the circumstances to them." She lifted a book that had been hidden in her lap. Recognizing what it was, I paled.

"I understand you allowed Travis York to remove this book from my library without my permission," she continued.

"I know I shouldn't have," I muttered.

"However, you did. Now here is the book, but where is the medallion that belongs inside?"

I swallowed. "Travis said he lost it last night on—on Mount Sangre."

"I suspected as much and have sent Jed to search for the medallion. Before he left, he brought me this." She lifted a tissue-paper-wrapped rectangle from her lap and laid it on the table. "Does it belong to you?"

Knowing it must be Luis's gift that I'd left at the barn, I nodded.

"Then please remove it from my sight. I will not be extending you any further invitations to Bloodstone House." She flicked her hand at me, much in the same way she used to dismiss her cat. "That will be all."

I rose. "I—I'm sorry," I mumbled.

"It's far too late for excuses. Goodbye, Valora."

Inexplicable tears filled my eyes as I murmured my farewell to her, picked up the book and exited. I couldn't understand why the tears since I couldn't wait to leave the horror of what happened behind me.

When in my room, I unwrapped Luis's gift—a small volume of poetry. I opened it to the inscription, Happy Eighteenth Birthday To Valora From Luis, and began to weep in earnest. As my great-aunt had said, it was too late to be sorry. Wanting no reminders of Luis or Travis, I left the book behind without reading even one of the poems.

My mother and stepfather left in September for a several-year stay in London and I went off to the University of California at Santa Cruz at the same time. The day before Christmas, Willa showed up at the apartment I shared with another student.

Though going to college had distracted me from brooding over what had happened on Mount Sangre, I couldn't forget that night and often had bad dreams. Seeing Willa brought it all back full force, especially when I saw the condition she was in.

"Your great-aunt blames me for getting pregnant," Willa said. "I tried to tell her I don't know how it happened—I swear Jack and me never went all the way—but she wouldn't believe me. Jack's mad at me, too. He says the kid's sure as hell not his and he won't have anything to do with me. No one will help me. I don't even have a place to live.''

My apartment-mate was sympathetic to Willa's plight so we took her in. But I found Willa changed— a ghost of the girl I used to know. She claimed she remembered nothing at all about the night on Mount Sangre.

''I lost my ring that night,'' she told me mournfully. ''The one you gave me, my lucky ring with the beautiful cat's-eye. My luck has been bad ever since.''

Otherwise, she refused to talk about the night. I didn't know what to believe. Unless Jack was lying, he wasn't the baby's father. That left either Travis or Luis to blame. I could only hope I'd never have to see them again.

''I want you to be the baby's guardian after I have her,'' Willa insisted and wouldn't be satisfied until I consulted a lawyer and made the arrangements ahead of time.

She delivered her daughter on March twenty-ninth and died the next day, holding my hand.

''I was always sorry I never had anything nice to give you,'' Willa whispered at the last.

Tears choked me, making me unable to answer, for I knew Willa was dying and leaving a gift behind for me, a gift beyond price—Tibbie. I was sure I'd never receive anything that meant more to me, but at the same time I realized the gift of Tibbie meant I could never entirely put the past behind me.

CHAPTER SIX

A tear squeezed its way from under my closed eyelids and trickled down my cheek as I relived Willa's death.

"Valora," Luis said softly, "what's wrong?"

I opened my eyes to the stone-bound sanctuary and to Luis leaning toward me. He raised his forefinger and wiped away the tear.

"I was remembering Willa dying," I whispered. "She saw Tibbie only once before—" I couldn't go on.

Luis gathered me to his side and I laid my head against his shoulder, fighting sobs.

"I had such a tough time hacking it in premed without any other responsibilities," he said, "that I wondered how you could possibly raise a child all alone while you were going to college. How *did* you manage?"

Sympathy would have had me weeping all over his shirt, but his matter-of-fact query dried my tears. I raised my head and pulled away, suddenly conscious of the two girls dabbling in the pool.

He let me go but kept his arm lightly around my shoulders. "Good friends and support from my mother and stepfather helped a lot," I told him. "My folks thought I was crazy, but they sent extra money when I needed it and there was always a friend willing to baby-sit. Tibbie did her part by being a great kid who loved everybody."

"It still couldn't have been easy."

"Didn't someone say nothing worthwhile is ever easy?"

Luis glanced at the girls. "Tibbie certainly seems healthy and happy."

This could have been my cue to mention her strange malady but I decided to hold my tongue. If none of the specialists who'd seen and examined Tibbie could come up with a reason for the spells, I couldn't expect Luis to. Even if he might be her father.

That thought forced me to my feet, away from the comfort of Luis's touch. I tried to conceal my abrupt movement by stretching as though I'd been sitting too long.

He rose, apparently unaware of my withdrawal. "Tibbie looks very much like Willa," he said.

I nodded. "Her hair's quite a bit darker but otherwise, yes."

My gaze slid over the raven blackness of Luis's hair. Travis was almost as blond as Willa had been and Jack, as nearly as I could recall, had lightish hair, too.

Willa had been an orphan, I reminded myself, so it was impossible to tell what color hair her parents and grandparents might have had.

He was looking at the girls, not me, and, when I saw him smile, I glanced at them. Hand in hand, they were wading in the pool, laughing and splashing.

"Spirit-sisters," Luis said.

I thought he might be right. Tibbie was a friendly child, but I'd never seen her take to anyone so quickly.

"It happens, you know," Luis went on, as though feeling he had to convince me. "My people believe these attachments are for a reason and encourage them. The tie is sometimes closer than with blood relatives.''

"Soso's a bright and attractive girl."

"Grandfather says she has a talent for healing—he's already teaching her what he knows."

"The way he taught you?" I asked.

"Not quite the same way. In my case, he tried to teach me more than healing, but my years in college and med school interfered."

"Didn't Running Fox want you to be a doctor?"

"When my chance came, he encouraged me. Grandfather's well aware of the desperate need our people have for the miracles of modern medicine— who better to bring them to the Miwok than one of the blood, is the way he figured it. But being a doctor leaves me little time to also be a Miwok shaman and he knows it."

I stared at him in surprise. "You, a shaman?"

Luis shrugged and dismissed the subject. "I'll bring Soso into town to visit Tibbie when I can," he said.

"I imagine they'll both like that. If her parents don't mind, there's no reason Soso can't spend the night when she visits."

"No problem."

Despite the sycamore's shade, I'd begun to feel the heat. Valley summers are *hot*. I wiped my forehead with a tissue, saying, "I could use a bit of cooling off."

"Let's join the girls in the pool for a game of Gotcha," he suggested, grinning. I agreed enthusiastically.

Some time later, with the four of us more or less soaked to the skin from the splashing game, Luis announced it was time to go because he had evening rounds to make. Naranada had no hospital, so his patients had to be sent to the I. R. Thompson Hospital in Thompsonville, a twenty-minute drive.

After we left Soso in the Miwok village, Tibbie dozed off in the back. Luis drove in silence for a while, no doubt enjoying the feel of the warm breeze against wet clothing as I was.

"How long do you plan to stay in town?" he asked finally.

I tensed, not caring to hear another argument about leaving. "Until Tibbie's school opens in September," I said guardedly.

He slanted me a one-sided smile. "Do you really expect me to behave that long?"

I was caught unaware by the wave of desire that washed through me, leaving me shaken by its intensity as the wish came unbidden that he'd stop behaving.

Pulling myself together, I shut away my need. I couldn't allow such feelings while the grim specter of the past haunted me.

"That's your problem," I said tartly.

"Wrong. As long as you remain here it's *our* problem. The other night in the gazebo showed us both that the heat when we come together has damn well blazed into a forest fire. I know the feeling scared you when you were eighteen, but you aren't a kid any longer. And neither am I."

"I'm quite capable of handling *my* emotions." I spoke through tight lips. "Tend to your own."

He didn't reply for so long I shot a glance at him, and found him grinning at me. "Stop trying to pull a Miss Faith act," he said, "and be honest."

"If this is another way of trying to convince me to leave Naranada, I don't find it amusing."

His grin faded abruptly. "I've given that up. Your dreams, along with the warning feathers, have convinced me you and Tibbie wouldn't be safe anywhere."

"But why?" I cried. "Tell me—"

"Why are you shouting, Mom?" Tibbie asked sleepily from the back. "Are you and Luis having a fight?"

"Sort of," Luis told her, "but it's nothing to worry about."

"I'd rather listen to the radio than to arguing," Tibbie told him.

"Done." Luis flicked on the radio, changing stations until he found rock music Tibbie not only approved of but began singing along with. To my annoyance he joined in. Was there anything Luis didn't know?

They sang and I fumed all the way back to town.

Luis dropped us off at Bloodstone House with a jaunty "See you," and drove away.

After Tibbie went to bed, I changed into my nightgown and lay on my bed reading a paperback, determined not to dwell on Luis's cryptic warning. Finally I grew drowsy and shut off the light. I fell asleep immediately.

The sun's rising rays slanting through my windows roused me. I sat up, aware of a strong lily of the valley scent in my room, a scent that gradually faded as I tried in vain to recall my dreams. When I saw no feather on the bedcovers I breathed a sigh of relief. Too soon. There on the floor at my feet was a gray-blue feather. At the same time, words echoed in my mind, words I vaguely recalled my great-aunt had said in last night's dream: *Beware a clever thief.*

I picked up the feather, turning it in my fingers. From a blue jay, I decided. In the Sierras the jays were called camp robbers because of their habit of darting down from the pines and flying off with morsels of any food in sight.

My fingers were steady as I placed the feather in the drawer with the other two. Finding it upset me, but I'd expected this one, I realized. Hadn't Running Fox said there'd be four in all? That left a final feather to go. I was far from sure whether or not he could read meaning into the feathers, but somehow I believed he was right in his prediction. Four feathers, no more and no less. I hoped the warning dreams would cease at the same time.

As for where the feathers came from, though I wasn't ready to accept supernatural causes, I had to admit it seemed unlikely that a hummingbird, a red-winged blackbird and a jay had not only flown down my chimney and into my room but had also managed to find their way out again, leaving behind no more than one feather apiece.

I mistrusted the intangible and was unhappy about being forced to face that what I'd always believed to be impossible might, after all, be true. I didn't want to be shown things existed beyond what I thought of as reality.

Tibbie bounced into my room. "I'm going to ride Misty right after breakfast," she announced. "Jed says I'm good enough so he can trust me alone if I don't take her far. I'll stay close and I promise not to ride on any of the roads. Okay?"

I nodded. Tibbie could be relied on to keep her word. As she hurried into her own room to dress, it crossed my mind that she hadn't had a spell since coming here other than that first one. I'd been disappointed too many times to allow myself to believe she might never have another, but I was glad there'd only been the one.

Jed had been told of her problem and I was sure he'd keep an eye on her even though allowing her the illusion of riding alone. And I'd keep trying my best to allow her some freedom despite my worries.

"Don't hover over her," her last psychologist had warned, "or Tibbie will feel smothered and wind up with more problems than having these spells."

After breakfast, Tibbie raced from the house, tossing a "'Bye, Mom," over her shoulder. Assuring myself she'd be just fine, I decided to return to my task of cataloging the Rolland library. In no time at all, I was thoroughly engrossed and was struck with surprise when I heard the hall clock strike eleven.

Two and a half hours had passed. Tibbie rarely rode Misty more than an hour—she should have returned to the house by now. Of course, she could be following Jed around as he worked; she liked the crusty old handyman. Still, I'd better check.

I left the house through the kitchen door just as Jed came limping up the flagstone walk.

"Your little gal ain't come back, Miss Valora," he said. "She told me she weren't taking the pony past the meadow. I kept my eye on her for a bit till I saw she meant it, but then I got to making them repairs I been putting off, on the corral fence, and when I looked again I couldn't find hide nor hair of her. Or the pony, neither."

A cold fist closed around my heart, but I tamped down my rising panic and asked, "Where did you last see her?"

"Right by the meadow, 'twas, near that little grove of figs."

The meadow was where she'd gone the last time she had a spell. Travis had found her in the old shed that had once sheltered him and Luis and me from the rain, the shed near the foot of Mount Sangre.

Without another word, I skirted around Jed and raced toward the meadow. Please let her be all right, let her be safe, I prayed as I ran. Her wandering off was always frightening. In Santa Cruz I worried about a possible child molester finding her. Here in Naranada I feared a more intangible menace, one whose nature I didn't know.

Halfway across the meadow, I caught sight of Misty ambling toward me, obviously heading back to the corral. She was riderless.

"Tibbie!" I cried, increasing my pace. "Tibbie, where are you?"

Though aware Tibbie wouldn't hear my shouts if she was locked into her spell, there was the chance she wasn't in a trance but had fallen off the pony and hurt herself.

There was no response to my shouts. Tense with apprehension, I reached the shed and plunged inside, searching. Tibbie wasn't there. When I emerged, I stared up at Mount Sangre, the metallic tang of fear sour on my tongue. There was no way to know if Tibbie had climbed that hill unless I went up there and looked for her. But when I tried to force myself to start climbing, my feet wouldn't move.

Until that moment, I hadn't realized just how terrified I was of Mount Sangre.

"Tibbie!" I screamed in desperation.

As my cry echoed from the foothills beyond, I thought I heard an answering shout. Holding my breath, I listened, and then spotted movement near the top of Mount Sangre, a man waving. Was that a child with him? Was it Tibbie?

"She's with me," he called, and I recognized Luis's voice.

With Luis. Why? Fury erased my fear. Why in God's name, after all his warnings, had Luis taken my daughter up there?

Still not able to convince myself to climb, I waited impatiently for them to reach the bottom of the hill. Tibbie ran down the last few feet and, as she rushed toward me, I saw she carried an animal of some kind.

"Mom, I found a kitten," she cried. "Can I keep him?"

"May I," I corrected automatically, putting my arm around her, all the while frowning at Luis.

"May I?" she persisted.

"I'll see. Right now I'm upset. You frightened me by going off without telling me. When I saw Misty without a rider I didn't know what to think."

I felt her tense under my hand. "I couldn't tell you," she mumbled.

"Why didn't you let me know?" I asked Luis angrily as he ambled up to us.

"Let you know what?"

"That you intended to take my daughter up Mount Sangre. Of all the—"

"Calm down," he advised. "I didn't take her anywhere. I saw Tibbie climbing the hill alone and went after her."

I stared at him. "What were you doing here in the first place?"

"Returning from a call. I have a few housebound patients who can't make it into the office—one of them lives between here and the York ranch."

"Mom," Tibbie said in a small voice, "it happened again. I don't remember getting off Misty, I don't even know where I found the kitten—I was holding him when I came out of it."

"Shall we walk back to your house?" Luis asked.

Numbly I nodded. Another spell. And this time she'd gone farther than the shed, this time she'd climbed Mount Sangre.

We passed Jed on the way back.

"She's all right, then," he said.

Again I nodded, not able to face the effort of explaining at the moment. I'd talk to Jed later. The three of us reached the house without another word being spoken and entered through the kitchen door, Luis coming in as though he'd been invited.

"Here you are, safe and sound," Delia said. "What's that you're carrying? A kitten, is it?"

Tibbie held out the little cat for Delia's inspection.

"Why it's the spittin' image of Sombra," Delia said.

I'd paid little attention to the kitten, but now that I noticed the markings—black with a white mask—I saw Delia was right.

"Can—may I keep him?" Tibbie asked again.

"I don't mind," Delia said, "but it's up to your mother."

"Yes, he can stay here," I said. "But right now I want you to go to your room and rest. I'll bring a lunch tray up in a bit—okay?"

Tibbie didn't argue. Clutching the squirming kitten to her, she hurried to the back stairs. Though I knew her quick obedience was in the hope I wouldn't notice she was taking the kitten upstairs with her, I said nothing. This one time it wouldn't hurt, and I thought she needed the comfort of the cat.

"Is the doctor staying to lunch?" Delia asked.

I glanced inquiringly at Luis.

He looked at his watch. "Much as I'd like to stay, I have office patients waiting. What I do need is a lift to where I left my car."

I agreed to give him a ride.

"Tell me about Tibbie," he said as we walked to the garage. "Do you know what's wrong with her?"

"No one's ever made a diagnosis. I've heard educated guesses that ran the gamut from petit mal epilepsy with fugue states to an unconscious search for her birth mother. All I know is she slips out of reality, wanders off, and when she comes back to herself she can't remember anything she did or why."

"She was mumbling, 'Where is it?' when I caught up to her," Luis said. "She'd already found the cat somewhere because she was carrying it. I realized she was in something resembling a fugue state. Since I didn't think it was a good idea for her to be on Mount Sangre, I took her hand and began leading her down. Almost immediately she said, 'I can't find it,' blinked and then spoke my name. After that she behaved normally. Did you ever have an EEG run to check her brain waves?"

Tibbie had suffered through three electroencephalograms as well as a CAT scan and MRI. "Every test is normal," I said wearily.

As we climbed into my car, Luis said, "Grandfather would say she's spirit-driven."

A glance showed me that his face was as serious as his tone of voice. I waited until I'd driven out of the garage to ask, "Would you believe him if he said that?"

"Considering the circumstances, I might. Willa was never the same after that night on Mount Sangre."

I slammed on the brakes, stopping the car so abruptly that only the seat belts kept us from being thrown forward. "You can't mean you think Tibbie's possessed by this—this darkness you seem to believe was set free."

"There's nothing of darkness in Tibbie, nothing evil."

I drove on slowly, still upset. "Then what are you talking about?"

"Spirit-driven, in Tibbie's case, means that she's compelled by something—let's call it a force—separate from her to search until she finds whatever it is this outside force wants or needs. If this is true, Willa's spirit may be responsible."

Half of me couldn't accept what he said, but the other half whispered, *Is it possible Tibbie's looking for her father?*

If she was, wouldn't that mean neither Travis nor Luis could be her father? After all, she'd encountered both of them while in one of her spells.

I shook my head. Luis's Miwok beliefs were too alien for me to accept. I could understand why he might think as he did, but I couldn't come to grips with the idea of spirits or outside forces. Willa was dead and ghosts didn't exist.

"Watch her, Valora," Luis warned. "Watch Tibbie closely and carefully, particularly until you leave Naranada."

Luis and I agreed absolutely on this one thing, if nothing else. "Yes," I said. "Yes, I will."

When I pulled onto the shoulder and stopped behind Luis's car, he turned to me, cupped my face between his hands and brushed his lips across mine. I don't know whether or not he meant it to be a casual goodbye kiss but, if he did, he was way off base.

As the kiss deepened, I lost all sense of the traffic passing on the county road beside us; my world was filled with his scent, with his taste, with the wonder of his mouth covering mine.

All too soon he pulled away, still cupping my face, his dark eyes half-closed as they gazed into mine. "Why did you tell me ten years ago you never wanted to see me again?" he asked huskily. "And why the hell did I believe you?"

He flung himself from my car before I'd recovered enough to speak. Needing a few moments to get my heartbeat back to normal, I waited, watching him slide into his own car and roar off down the road.

Ten years ago I'd put everything and everyone in Naranada behind me, determined never to return. Yet here I was.

Willa and my great-aunt were gone forever, but Luis was still here, as was Travis. And so was Bloodstone House and Mount Sangre. Involuntarily I turned my head to look at that damned hill, a fair distance away. My view of the lower half was cut off by the lemon grove alongside the road—the shed and the meadow were completely hidden by the trees.

Luis, I thought, must have cut through the grove to reach Mount Sangre after he'd parked and it would have taken him several minutes even if he ran. I frowned, wondering how, from this far, he'd been so certain it was Tibbie he saw on the hill.

And then I wondered how I could be sure he'd been telling me the truth.

Could anyone connected with that night on Mount Sangre ever be trusted?

CHAPTER SEVEN

The next morning, after a troubled dream where I wept over a closed coffin, I woke to the sound of Tibbie chanting in a singsong cadence:

"I have seen the footprints
Of those who lonely-walk
When night coils round
The silent places . . ."

I sat up abruptly. "What on earth are you reading?" I asked, looking down to where she sat crosslegged on the floor beside my bed.

"A poem called 'Ghosts Leave No Tracks' in this book Luis gave you when you were a teenager. It's about Indians, I guess. I don't really understand them, but the words kind of make me shiver, you know?"

I knew. But I wasn't thinking of Indians, I was remembering how malignant darkness had coiled around me that night on Mount Sangre. . . .

"I thought maybe reading poetry to you would be a nice way for you to wake up," she added. Putting a marker between the pages, she started to close the book.

"Wait a minute. What's that you're using for a bookmark?" I asked.

"Just a feather I found on the floor by your bed."

I held out my hand and she gave me the book. Opening it, I removed a brown feather spotted with black. I didn't recognize the bird the feather came from as I quickly slid it into the drawer with the others.

"That's the second feather I found in here," Tibbie said, climbing onto my bed. "Are birds really coming down the chimney into your fireplace?"

Since I didn't want to talk about the feathers or how they came to be in my room, I distracted her by saying, "Do I hear a scratching at the door?"

"Diablo!" she cried, jumping down, running to my door and flinging it open.

To my surprise, since I'd only pretended to hear a noise, the little cat, tail upraised, marched into the room as if he owned the place.

Tibbie lifted him into her arms and brought him to my bed. "Delia says Great-aunt Faith's cat must have been his grandmother or maybe his great-grandmother. Did Sombra really look exactly like him?"

"As nearly as I can recall." I plucked the kitten from my pillow and set him on the floor. He promptly began to climb up the quilt. "Diablo certainly seems to feel at home here."

"I don't think he was anyone's pet 'cause he's awful thin. Delia said he must have been real hungry 'cause he ate enough for a cat twice his size."

Knowing what she was really asking, I said, "We'll have to take him to a vet for his shots, but I don't see any reason you can't keep him unless someone advertises for a lost kitten and describes him. In that case we'd have to return Diablo to his rightful owner."

"I suppose. But I think Diablo found me 'cause he wanted to be my cat." Tibbie stroked his back and he climbed into her lap, purring. "Now I won't ever be alone again."

"Oh, sweetie," I said, stricken. "You aren't alone, you've got me."

She smiled at me as though she were the adult and I the child. "I know *that*. But you're my mother and mothers have to love their kids. No one else has to love me, only if they want to. Diablo needed someone to love so he found me."

I hugged her, touched by her words, and wished the world were as simple as Tibbie saw it.

As we were eating breakfast, the phone rang.

"Dr. Redhawk," Delia reported.

"I'm making a call in the Miwok village this morning," he said when I came on the line. "If it's all right with you, I thought I'd bring Soso back with me."

"Tibbie will be thrilled," I assured him.

"I'll drop her off sometime before noon, then." He said goodbye and hung up.

I set the phone down, resting my hand on it, wondering why I felt vaguely disappointed. Had I expected him to add something more personal?

Before I could move, the phone rang again, startling me. Luis, with something he'd forgotten to say to me? I picked it up, my hello slightly breathless.

"Travis here. How does lunch today in Visalia sound?"

Recovering quickly, I said, "Not today, I'm afraid. Tibbie's having a friend come to visit."

"To tell the truth, I wasn't planning to invite your daughter, charming as she is. I was thinking in terms of the two of us."

"I can't go off and leave Delia to look after the two girls. And to be honest, Travis, even if Soso wasn't coming today, I'd have to refuse. This is Tibbie's summer so I'm afraid she and I are a package deal when it comes to invitations."

"What, no wicked and decadent nightlife for you alone?"

I laughed. "I doubt that Naranada has any to offer."

"Tell me this—how in hell is a guy supposed to woo you with a child underfoot?"

"Maybe I'd rather not be wooed." I spoke lightly, matching his tone.

"Ah, fair lady, you've broken my heart. But, since you refuse to lunch with me, I suppose that, broken heart and all, I'll have to coax an invitation to lunch from you. How about it?"

"If you think you can bear two little girls underfoot, by all means join us."

"*Muchas gracias,* my lovely, if reluctant, señorita. I shall come bearing gifts."

I was still smiling when I returned to the kitchen where Tibbie and I were having breakfast. I found it much cozier there, as well as less trouble for Delia, since she insisted on serving us. After her first protest—"Miss Faith would turn over in her grave if she knew"—Delia made no other objection to our eating in the kitchen.

"I've invited Mr. York to lunch," I told Delia, "so we'll be four, with Soso. Nothing elaborate."

"Soso's coming?" Tibbie cried. "Great!"

While Delia and I discussed the lunch menu, Tibbie began planning out loud all the things she and Soso would do.

Later Tibbie, with the kitten in her arms, trailed me into the library. Diablo yowled, struggled free of her hold, leaped to the floor where, fur raised, he spat toward the fireplace, slowly backing away until he reached the door. There he turned and fled. Tibbie ran after him.

I crossed to the fireplace and looked inside. Since it was summer, the grate was clean and the vents closed. I couldn't imagine what had upset the kitten. I stared at the heavy wooden panels that edged the marble facade of the fireplace and rose to support the elaborate walnut mantel. Hideous as the carved griffins on the panels were, I doubted a cat would notice such things.

No outside odor should have filtered in to bother Diablo since the windows were closed because the air-conditioning was on, central air being one of my great-aunt's rare grudging concessions to the modern world. I wondered how my ancestors who'd lived in Bloodstone House in earlier days had borne the summer heat of the valley without this convenience.

To the best of my recollection, Sombra had never avoided the library when I visited my great-aunt as a girl. Diablo had made himself at home in the rest of the house—what did he find threatening here?

"I've come—reluctantly, mind you—to believe cats see beyond us, beyond our feeble senses," I remembered Great-aunt Faith telling me once. "Sombra quite unsettles me at times."

I shook my head, refusing to believe Diablo had sensed something past my ability to understand. He was young, and kittens, I reassured myself, were apt to take fright easily.

Tibbie didn't return, and when I went in search of her I found her at the top of the front staircase with Diablo chasing her jacks ball as it bounced from step to step. He captured it when the ball reached the entry floor.

"I thought you were going to help me in the library until Soso arrived," I said.

"Diablo doesn't like it in there."

Thinking he might be over his fright, I retrieved the ball from the kitten and rolled it across the polished parquet toward the library. He dashed in pursuit, but, when the ball rolled into the library, Diablo stopped short at the doorway.

"See?" Tibbie said.

Abandoning the idea of working in the library because after yesterday's fright I wouldn't be comfortable unless I was within sight or sound of Tibbie, I said, "Let's take a walk in the grape arbor while we wait. Diablo might enjoy an outing."

She nodded, gathering up the kitten.

The shade in the arbor was welcome as we walked under the burgeoning grapevines. I noticed that the white flowers of the Thompson Seedless had crumpled and disappeared, leaving green nubbins that would grow and swell into lusciously sweet fruit by August. Tibbie was more interested in watching Diablo try in vain to catch a white butterfly.

"What would he do with the butterfly if he caught it?" she asked.

"Probably eat it."

"Ugh, how gross."

"Cats are born to be hunters. In the wild, if they didn't hunt and eat what they captured, they'd starve. Diablo doesn't have to hunt for his food, but he will anyway because he's a cat and it's his nature." I didn't go into how cats often toyed with their captured prey before eating it, figuring I'd field that one only when I was forced to.

Thinking of prey reminded me of seeing the owl kill Willa's kitten years before, and I said, "We must be careful to keep Diablo inside at night until he's full grown and able to take care of himself."

Tibbie nodded vigorously. "Jed showed me the pine tree where a white owl roosts in the daytime. He told me owls hunt from dusk to dawn and they kill and eat any little animals they can find."

Taken aback, I said, "You mean you saw an owl on our property?"

"He was hidden in the branches so all I could see was a few white feathers. But I noticed this junk under the tree—pellets, Jed calls them." She grimaced. "He said the pellets are rolled-up fur and pieces of bones and stuff the owl can't digest. That old owl's not getting hold of my Diablo!"

Speaking of the owl made me uneasy, though this bird couldn't possibly be the same one—or could it? I had no idea how long owls lived. It upset me to think the owl might be the one whose white feather, on that fateful night, had spiraled down into the circle of blood on the stone....

Enough of owls!

"Let's go back to the house and get some bread to feed to the ducks." I forced cheerfulness into my voice.

"I'd rather wait till I can show Soso the ducks," Tibbie said.

Realizing what she really wanted to do was watch for Soso's arrival, I said, "How about playing catch with a tennis ball in the front while we wait?"

"I'll get the ball," Tibbie said, running toward the house.

Later, after retrieving the ball for the fourth or fifth time, she complained, "How come it's always me that misses, not you?"

"You play the piano better than I do, already you can dance better, but don't forget I was captain of the girls' softball team in high school—leave me a little glory."

Tibbie drew her hand back to toss the ball, then paused, listening. "I think I hear a car turning into the driveway—maybe that's Soso coming now."

We walked to the edge of the grass and watched Luis's four-wheel drive swing around the circle and stop. Soso jumped out, waved back at the enthusiastically waving Tibbie, then stared solemnly at the house.

"Your house is like something on TV," Soso told Tibbie when we reached her.

"That's what I thought when I first saw it," Tibbie said. "How long can you stay?"

Soso glanced at Luis, who was walking around to where we stood.

"I told her grandmother she'd be back late tomorrow," Luis said. "Okay?"

"You mean Soso gets to stay all night?" When I nodded, Tibbie cried, "Yea!"

Luis reached into the car, removed what looked like a book pack and handed it to Soso.

"Come on," Tibbie said. "You can put your stuff in my room."

Watching the two girls run toward the house, I sighed. "I wish I could allow Tibbie more freedom while Soso's here but I'm afraid—"

"I told Soso about Tibbie," Luis said.

I stared at him. "You mean you discussed Tibbie's spells with her?"

He nodded. Before I could protest, he said, "Soso's not an ordinary little girl, she's in training to be a medicine woman and so she's learned to be responsible. She's already able to help Grandfather and that's saying a lot. Take it from one who knows, he's not easy to work with."

"But," I sputtered, "she'll think Tibbie's some kind of freak. It'll ruin their friendship."

"Nothing of the sort. Soso understands that Tibbie is as normal as she is except for an occasional spell. She knows if Tibbie begins to act odd and says, 'Where is it?' over and over that she must take Tibbie's hand and lead her to you. From my experience, in one of her spells Tibbie comes along willingly enough if taken by the hand."

"How can you expect a nine-year-old girl to make herself responsible for Tibbie?"

"Soso's a healer, Valora. By inclination and by training she has a need to help others. You can trust her with Tibbie. She told me herself that she and Tibbie 'see into the heart' of each other. I wouldn't be surprised if Tibbie decides to confide in her about the spells. In fact, I told Soso to simply listen if she does, not saying she already knows."

I bit my lip. "I hope you haven't done the wrong thing."

"I'm sure I haven't. I'll come by to pick up Soso tomorrow after office hours—which should be one, but more likely will be about three."

"Fine." I waited, wondering if he'd ask when he could see me again, but he merely gave me a quick smile and a nod. He was turning away when a fire red foreign sports car zoomed up the driveway, into the circle, and came to a dramatic halt.

Travis hopped out. "Just leaving, Luis?" he asked.

Luis nodded.

"We'll have to get together one of these days," Travis said.

"If you like." Luis's tone was neutral.

"Actually, I'm planning a party for later this month. I'll give you a ring." Travis seemed about to clap Luis on the shoulder but changed his mind at the last minute.

Despite Travis's apparent friendliness and Luis's impassivity, I sensed tension between the two men. Was it chronic or because of me?

Since when have you become a femme fatale? I asked myself. Travis and Luis never were buddies in the past, why should they be now?

Luis slid into his car and drove off.

"He always was one taciturn Indian," Travis said. "But then, most of them are."

"Not among friends," I said, put off by Travis's stereotyping.

Travis shrugged. "Obviously Luis likes you better than he does me. Not that I blame him—you're the prettiest gal I've ever met." He took my hand as we walked toward the house, swinging our clasped hands back and forth as though we were teenagers. Or lovers.

At the front door he stopped, turned to me and intoned, "The prettiest gal I ever met, is you, sweet Val, my Juliet."

I rolled my eyes. "Not that Romeo-Juliet business again."

He clutched his chest. "Is this the only thanks I get for my incomparable couplet?"

I couldn't help but be amused.

Lunch went well. Travis's attention to the girls succeeded in making Tibbie laugh, though he was able to coax only one sparse smile from Soso. I thought it might be because she was shy with adults she didn't know.

When dessert arrived—chocolate-chip cookies—Tibbie was discussing what our first names meant. "My mother's means powerful or valiant," she finished, her gaze on Travis. "Mr. York, what does your first name mean?"

He smiled. "Actually, Travis is a family last name, a shortened form of Travers, and my grandmother told me Travers meant a crossroads."

"You mean where two roads cross?" Tibbie asked.

He nodded. "My grandmother believed a crossroads was a spot to be avoided at night. In the old days in England, she said, they buried people suspected of being witches at a crossroads."

"You were named after a bad place," Soso put in—almost the first she'd spoken since we sat down to eat.

He looked solemnly at her. "If you could rename me, Soso, what name would you choose?"

Soso sat silent for so long I thought she wasn't going to answer. "There's a name among my people," she said at last. "Yutu." She spelled it out. "Maybe I'd pick that one."

"And what does Yutu mean?" Travis asked.

Soso bit her lip. "Coyote." Her voice was so low we hardly heard her.

Travis chuckled. "So I'm Coyote, am I? Unless I'm mistaken, he's some kind of a god in Indian mythology, right?"

He was looking at me when he asked, but Soso answered. "Sort of."

"I'd say being even sort of a god is better than being a mere mortal." Travis sounded strangely serious.

After we left the table, the girls, trailed by Diablo, went into the music room to play the piano and Travis and I drifted into the library.

"For some reason Tibbie's kitten's afraid to come into this room," I said idly.

"Really? Why do you think?"

Taken somewhat aback by his interest, I shrugged. "He's healthy enough according to the vet—maybe another cat could give a reason but I can't."

Travis began to prowl the room like a cat himself, his glance darting from wall to wall and from floor to ceiling.

"For heaven's sake, stop pacing," I said at last. "You're setting my teeth on edge."

"Do you realize how much you sound like your great-aunt at times?" he asked, stopping and leaning against the mantel. "Luckily, I'm more than willing to make certain you don't turn into her. All you have to do is to smile and say yes."

"Yes to what?"

"Pretend for a moment you're Juliet."

"And I suppose you're Romeo." I spoke dryly. "In that case, my answer is that we're too old to be playing childish games. Besides, since you and I are friends, there's nobody left to carry on the feud between the Yorks and the Rollands, hence no reason for me to pretend to be Juliet."

"Ah, but don't forget a Rolland still claims ownership of York land."

I frowned. "Claim isn't the right word. I legally own that piece of land."

"Putting aside the nefarious scheme your ancestors used to obtain the legal rights, can you honestly tell me you're proud to own Mount Sangre?"

I shuddered involuntarily.

"Then why not sell it to me and have it done?" he asked, the teasing note gone from his voice.

"Selling Mount Sangre doesn't remove that damned hill from my sight," I said heatedly.

"You're letting what happened in the past turn a mound of soil and rock into something monstrous. That's not reasonable, Val."

"Maybe not but I can't think why you'd want to buy such an ill-omened place."

"Because it's my family duty to reclaim York land. I got the impression you don't intend to live here—do you plan to hang on to the property indefinitely? Lease it, perhaps? I'd hate to see you rent Bloodstone House to strangers."

I shook my head, tamping down my rising irritation at his persistence. "We're beginning to sound like our feuding ancestors. To be honest, I don't yet know what my plans are. If I do decide to sell Bloodstone House and the rest of the property, Mount Sangre included, I promise you'll have first refusal."

"Mom," Tibbie said from the doorway, "I taught Soso to play the top part of 'Chopsticks' while I play the bottom—come listen to us."

"It seems our attendance is required at a concert of two talented pianists," Travis said, offering his arm to me. "May I be your escort?"

As Tibbie giggled, I took his arm, deciding it was impossible to stay annoyed at Travis.

He left not long after the "concert," reminding me before he said goodbye that he'd be calling me about the party he was planning. Then, because Tibbie was eager to show Soso the pony and the duck pond, the three of us toured the grounds. While they petted Misty, I spoke to Jed.

"It's too hot this afternoon, so I'll let them ride tomorrow morning," I told him, "but I want you to watch, okay?"

"Won't take my eyes off 'em," he assured me. "They're sure thick as thieves already, ain't they?"

In a roundabout way, his words reminded me that I'd forgotten to mention to Luis that I now had four feathers. Perhaps I ought to give them to Soso to take to Running Fox. Once I'd gotten rid of them, I might be able to stop puzzling over the riddle of how the feathers had gotten into my room and onto my bed while I slept.

When we returned to the house, the girls decided to play some of Tibbie's games up in her room and, after dinner, they watched television—yet another re-run of *The Wizard Of Oz*. Tibbie never tired of the movie and Soso had seen it only once before.

In the twilight, I wandered along the path toward the gazebo, now and then glimpsing the dark outline of Mount Sangre through the trees. Though I kept telling myself I'd look in the other direction, it seemed my eyes refused to see anything else. I stopped abruptly, staring, when a light winked on at the top of the hill. A moment later it was gone.

Had I imagined the light or was someone there? Mount Sangre was generally shunned by the locals.

Not only was it private land with a dark reputation, but a sort of invisible pall hung over the place, discouraging those who might decide to trespass. Once in a while a kid from town would climb the hill on a dare—during the daytime.

Naranada had no shortage of hills, and others were more welcoming to daylight picnickers and moonlight lovers. So if someone was on Mount Sangre this evening—who could it be?

I waited for what seemed hours but the light didn't return, making me uncertain I'd actually seen one in the first place. No longer wishing to visit the gazebo, I returned to the house in time to see the Wicked Witch melt into a putrid puddle while Tibbie and Soso cheered.

When I finally fell asleep that night, I dreamed I was wandering, like Dorothy, in a field of flowers. Not poppies, but lilies of the valley. The poppies of Oz might contain sleep magic in their perfume but these tiny white flowers surrounding me were more dangerous because they carried death in their delicate and poisonous fringed bells. And yet I was tempted beyond the power of resistance to pick and eat the beautiful and deadly little lilies.

Something invisible grabbed my arm, shaking me, calling my name, and suddenly I was free of the compulsion, free to—

"Valora," a voice whispered. "Wake up, Valora."

I roused with a start to find Soso standing beside my bed, her hand on my shoulder. Sitting up quickly, I said, "What's wrong? Is Tibbie—?"

"She's asleep. But I hear something downstairs, something moving around, and I'm scared."

I listened, hearing indeterminate noises that raised the hair on my nape. "Maybe Delia's up," I said, speaking to myself as much as to Soso.

"Wouldn't she be in the kitchen?" Soso whispered.

As near as I could tell, the sounds came from the front of the house rather than the rear, where the kitchen was. Gathering my courage, I rose, told Soso to stay where she was, tiptoed across to my bedroom door and eased it open. I edged into the hall, fearfully listening to scuffing noises. Something or someone *was* downstairs.

I swallowed, opened my mouth and called, "Delia, is that you?"

Total silence greeted me.

"Delia?" I called again, louder.

Much louder sounds, then the front door closed. I choked back the scream I knew would do nothing but scare the girls, inched along the wall until I found the switch at the head of the stairs and flicked on the upper hall lights.

"What's all the racket?" a voice demanded, startling me before I realized it was Delia speaking from the back of the hall. Knowing she was there made me braver.

"Someone was downstairs," I told her as she neared me. "I think he left by the front door."

Delia gaped at me. "But that door was locked tight as a tick. I checked it myself before I went to bed."

"I'd better have a look."

"You aren't going down those stairs without me along," Delia insisted.

The two of us descended with me in the lead, turning on the lights as I came to each switch.

Delia gasped as we reached the entry. "Lord Almighty, I swear I smell her perfume," she said.

I couldn't deny that the lily-of-the-valley scent, though faint, was pervasive.

"'Tis Miss Faith's ghost walking, sure as sin," Delia insisted, clutching my arm. "Mark my words, her ghost is still looking for whatever she couldn't find before she died."

"What I heard was no ghost!" Because her words had raised goose bumps on my arms, I spoke more sharply than I meant to.

"There!" Delia cried, pointing. "What's that I see moving?"

The library door, barely ajar, *was* moving, the gap widening.

CHAPTER EIGHT

Delia and I clung to each other as we watched the library door crack open. Though the entry hall was brightly lit, it did nothing to banish my fear of what might lie within the darkness of the library. What was pushing the door open? I tensed as something black poked through at the bottom of the gap.

"Lord save us, a snake," Delia whispered.

A moment later my pent-up breath whooshed out as Diablo's white mask appeared in the space between door and frame. The kitten squeezed through the opening and, ears laid back, ran as though for his life, skirting us to dash up the stairs.

"I left that cat closed in the storeroom off the kitchen," Delia said. "How'd he get loose?"

I disentangled myself from her and advanced toward the library, nervously pushing the door all the way open and turning on the light. No one was in the room, nor did it appear disturbed except for one book lying on the floor near the fireplace. But the lily-of-the-valley scent was stronger than ever.

"It's like I told you—Miss Faith's ghost." Delia spoke from behind me. "She let the cat out, maybe thinking he was Sombra, so he could help her search."

"Diablo's afraid of the library. He wouldn't come into this room willingly—not even for a ghost. And, if there are such things as ghosts, surely they wouldn't need to use doors to go in and out. I distinctly heard someone leave the house by the front door.''

Together we examined the door and found it locked.

"Someone must have an extra key,'' I said.

"I don't see how. I told you Miss Faith had the locks changed not long before she died and there was only three keys came with the locks. She had one, I had one and the third she kept in her room. I took that third key from her bedside stand after she died and hid it in a chest. The key I gave you was hers. So how could anyone have an extra key?''

"Maybe he doesn't,'' I said. "The intruder could have come in another way, unlocked the door to get out and then locked it behind him as he left. We'd better look for an unlocked or forced window.''

We checked every downstairs window and found all of them locked. The basement windows didn't open, I knew, and, though it wasn't impossible for a man— I couldn't imagine the prowler was a woman—with a ladder, I didn't think he'd gained entry from a second-floor window. In the morning we'd examine the basement and second-story windows to be sure all were intact.

"The silver's where it ought to be,'' Delia reported after a search of the dining room. "I can't see anything's missing, leastways nothing noticeable.''

As we stood in the entry debating what to do next, I heard a noise. Tensing, I looked up and saw Soso halfway down the steps with the kitten in her arms.

"It's all right,'' I assured her. "No one's in the house who shouldn't be.''

She nodded, turned and climbed the stairs, vanishing down the hall.

"Nothing more we can do tonight," Delia said. "Unless you mean to call the police."

Since our uninvited visitor apparently hadn't stolen anything, I didn't see much point in disturbing Naranada's one-man police force in the middle of the night. I thought it unlikely, with every light in the house on, that the intruder was likely to return between now and dawn. In any case, I planned to stay up and I suspected Delia did, too.

If in the morning we discovered evidence of a break-in or something did turn up missing, I'd talk to the police then.

But we did not. Every window in the place proved to be intact and, if anything was missing, neither Delia nor I knew what it could be. I felt she still clung to her ghost theory. I couldn't deny I'd also smelled the perfume my great-aunt habitually wore, but I'd also heard the front door close. Though I had no explanation for the lily-of-the-valley odor, I believed the intruder was human and a man.

Tibbie, a bit miffed because she'd slept through all the night's excitement, pounced eagerly on the book lying on the library floor. "It's a clue, Mom," she insisted. "Nancy Drew is always finding clues like this and solving the mystery."

"The intruder probably knocked that book off the table in passing," I said mildly.

"But it's still a clue. Just look at the title, *The Book of Birds.* And you've been finding feathers in your room."

I lifted the old brown book from her hands, noting it had been published by the National Geographic Society in 1921. When the book fell open to a remarkable-for-the-time flashlight photograph of a snowy owl, a frisson of fear shot along my spine.

Tibbie pointed to a gap in a row of books on a shelf. "See, here's where it must have come from, 'cause all the other books along here are about animals and birds."

I had to admit the feathers, the book and the unsettling picture of the owl did seem to be part of a whole—it was a remarkable coincidence, if nothing else. But if I accepted that the book had been deliberately taken from the shelf and dropped so I'd find the page with the owl, the next thing I knew, I'd be believing Delia's story about ghosts and be sure my great-aunt had come back from the dead to warn me.

Warn me of what? I shook my head.

"Aw, mom, it really *is* a clue," Tibbie said.

Hating to disappoint her, I said, "I'm not Nancy Drew so I don't understand what the book is a clue to. And if you and Soso are going to ride Misty this morning, you'd better get started. Jed's waiting in the kitchen."

Earlier, I'd told Jed I wanted dead bolts put on all the doors leading outside and he'd assured me he'd drive into town after the girls finished riding and buy the bolts. I hoped he'd have them in place before nightfall. I might not believe in ghosts, but the idea of a relative's ghost was less frightening than the thought of someone alive creeping into the house after dark, no matter what his reason might be.

Once the girls had gone off with Jed, I tried to make sense of what had happened the night before. Odd as it seemed, the intruder must have brought the kitten into the library with him. When I'd checked the storeroom windows—two small ones, high off the ground—I'd found them not only locked and intact but painted into immobility. They were impossible to open. Since I didn't doubt Delia had shut the kitten in the room for the night, that meant someone had deliberately opened the door and not only let Diablo out, but carried him into the library.

Delia had mentioned using the cat to help find something. She'd been talking about my great-aunt's ghost, not the intruder, but was it possible he'd hoped the kitten could locate some hidden object, an object he'd come to steal? The idea seemed farfetched, but the fact remained that the kitten had been taken into the library.

Weeks before she died, Great-aunt Faith had prowled the house at night searching for something she claimed she'd lost. She'd insisted the owl was calling her and, sadly, she'd died without finding what she sought. The owl medallion? Though Delia claimed she was sure Jed had retrieved the medallion ten years ago and returned it to my great-aunt, I decided to talk to him about it myself.

As far as I was concerned, the damned thing could stay hidden forever, but if someone unknown was slipping into Bloodstone House at night to search for God knows what, possibly it *was* the medallion he was after. But why now and not ten years ago? It didn't make sense.

One thing seemed obvious. There was no point in notifying the police when I had no real proof there'd even *been* an intruder.

Travis called around noon, wanting to discuss his upcoming party, but the strain I was under must have showed in my voice because almost immediately he asked me what was wrong.

"We had an intruder last night," I said.

"Damn! What happened? Never mind, I'm coming over to find out for myself."

He hung up before I could say another word.

I had to admit I was glad to see Travis even if all he actually did was go through the house searching for possible methods of entry. When he rejoined me in the morning room, he shook his head. "You're sure there's no extra key?" he asked.

I repeated what Delia had told me.

"If she knows what she's talking about, I don't understand how the bastard got in," he said. "Everyone knew Miss Faith was getting a bit dotty there at the end—it could be she secretly had a duplicate key made."

"Why would she?"

He shrugged. "Beats me. Sorry I don't have any other pearls to offer. When Jed gets those dead bolts on, you should be safe enough, but if you'd like me to spend the night—"

"No," I said hastily. "Thanks for the offer but, as you say, the dead bolts should be enough."

"I'll come back later this afternoon and see how everything is." He gave me a quick hug before leaving.

At two Luis called and said he'd had an emergency so he wouldn't be driving to the Miwok village until Sunday and he hoped it wasn't inconvenient for me to keep Soso one more night.

"As long as her people won't be upset," I said, preparing to tell him what had happened during the night.

"I'll let Grandfather know," Luis said. "Sorry, I have to run. I'll try to stop by this evening, but I can't promise I'll make it." He hung up before I had the chance to let him know about the intruder.

Tibbie was delighted to hear Soso was staying on. Soso, though agreeable, was less enthusiastic, and I knew she was wondering what threat the night might bring to Bloodstone House.

I was somewhat apprehensive myself. Jed hadn't been able to find dead bolts in the local general store and had driven into Visalia to look for them, at least an hour each way, probably longer in his battered old pickup. Still, he should return in time to install the bolts before dark.

Travis returned at five, frowning when he heard Jed wasn't back yet from Visalia. "I'll be glad to stay," he repeated. "I could bed down on the leather couch in the library and—"

"Really, it's not necessary. We'll have the new bolts and I'll leave lights on downstairs." Though I appreciated Travis's concern and his offer, it was my problem, not his.

"Promise you'll call me if you need me."

I promised him. He took another turn through the house before he left, assuring me every window was shut and locked.

My next phone call came from Jed, just after seven. He'd bought the bolts, but his truck had broken down.

"They promised it'd be ready by noon tomorrow," he said. "Ain't nothing I can do but spend the night here in Visalia."

"I could drive over and get you," I offered nervously.

"Now don't you bother doing no such thing. Them bolts can wait. What you want to do tonight is ram a chair under every one of them doorknobs. That'll hold okay temporary-like. Anyways, whoever he is, if he comes back two nights in a row he's as crazy as a steer that's been chawing on locoweed.''

Resigned to the temporary measures Jed had suggested, if not overjoyed about his picture of a deranged prowler, I was about to hang up when I remembered my question and so I asked him.

"Yeah, I found what Miss Faith sent me after," he replied, obviously not happy about discussing the matter. "And I gave it to her. She was a sly boots, she was. Don't know what she did with the thing and don't want to know.''

Since I thought it might make the girls feel more secure if they knew what we were doing to keep the house safe, I made a game out of finding exactly the right kind of chair to fit under the knob of each door. Then I let them test the arrangement on an inside door so they could discover for themselves how well a chair held a door closed. Soso treated it less like a game than Tibbie, but afterward I thought she seemed satisfied.

The only problem was the French doors off the morning room, which opened out rather than in like the others. But, since they had ordinary bolts at the top and the bottom that held the two doors together when they were closed, I decided not to worry about them. True, a determined intruder could smash his way in, but I felt the man who'd been in my library the night before preferred the secrecy of silence and stealth and wouldn't resort to smashing glass or splintering wood.

Nevertheless, though I didn't mention it to anyone, I intended to sit up all night. I'd been looking forward to seeing Luis but, when he hadn't arrived by ten, I realized he wouldn't be coming. Delia refused to retire until I did, and, since I feared she'd insist on sharing the vigil with me if she knew what I planned, I pretended to go to bed.

When I looked in to make sure the girls were asleep, Diablo lifted his head from Tibbie's pillow to stare at me. I'd decreed that the kitten couldn't share her bed at night but there he was. Before I came up, she must have sneaked down the back stairs and rescued Diablo from his nightly exile to the utility room. I thought about removing him but finally decided that maybe tonight both girls needed the extra comfort a purring kitten could provide. The vet had assured me the cat was healthy and I probably was being too finicky.

Once I was certain Delia must be sleeping, too, I rose, pulled a robe over my nightgown and crept apprehensively down the stairs. An old house is never completely silent. Between the ticks of the hall clock I heard various creaks and pings, not alarming but adding to my foreboding. At least I wasn't descending into the dark, for I'd left the lights on in the dining room, the library and outside the front door. As I reached the entry, a flash of headlights told me a car had pulled into the driveway. I stared from one of the long windows framing the door and recognized Luis's four-wheel drive.

By the time he reached the steps, I'd pulled the chair from under the knob, unlocked the door and opened it. My relief at seeing him must have been apparent, because after one look at my face, he pushed the door shut, wrapped his arms around me and held me close.

For long moments I felt safe and protected, then the bong of the clock chiming eleven startled me.

"You're jumpy," he said, gazing down at me. "What's the matter?"

I eased from his arms. "Come into the library and I'll tell you."

Once there, he pulled me down beside him on the couch. Reminding myself it wasn't wise to trust Luis too much, I curled into one corner and began. He watched me as I spoke, frowning occasionally but showing no other emotion.

"Soso heard him before you did?" he asked after I finished.

"Yes, and when I thought about it later I was a little surprised, because I'm a very light sleeper."

"I wonder if she heard him first or sensed him first."

I blinked. Sensed the intruder? What could he mean?

He unhooked his beeper and set it on the lamp table. "Unless I get an emergency call, I'm staying here for the rest of the night."

"Really, Luis," I began, "it's not—"

"Don't argue, you have no grounds. Why haven't you heeded the warnings? Don't you understand that danger now stalks you in your own home?"

Though his words chilled me, I fought back. "I don't think the intruder was after me, I believe he was searching for something," I said stubbornly. "Something in this room."

Luis's glance swept the bookshelves.

"Not a book," I said. "Though I haven't finished cataloging them all yet, I'm positive Great-aunt Faith didn't leave anything on the shelves even remotely resembling that horrible grimoire we took up Mount Sangre ten years ago. Delia said my great-aunt burned that and several other books soon afterward."

"Grimoire," Luis repeated. "I'd never even heard the word before that night."

"I'd just as soon never say or hear it again."

"What about the owl medallion?" Luis asked.

"No one knows where it is. Delia says my great-aunt searched through every trunk and chest in the house before she died. After her death, Delia hired Lucy Jennings and her two teenage daughters to clean Bloodstone House from top to bottom. Attic, basement, nothing was overlooked."

Luis leaned his head against the high back of the couch and closed his eyes. Only then did I notice how tired he looked. I wondered when he'd last slept or eaten.

"Would you like some food?" I asked belatedly.

"I wouldn't turn down a sandwich and coffee."

When I returned to the library, I was pushing a serving cart loaded with coffee, ham slices, homemade dinner rolls warmed in the microwave and what was left of the peanut butter cookies topped with chocolate Delia had baked for the girls. I found Luis as I'd left him but now sound asleep.

Unbidden, a fantasy unrolled in my inner vision, a fantasy about Luis I thought I'd left behind in my teenage years.

Wearing nothing but a light cotton halter dress and panties, I ventured into the garden in the late afternoon, hoping Luis hadn't yet left for the day. Knowing I was safe from my great-aunt's prying eyes because she'd left to dine at a friend's house made me bold and I was determined that, whatever might happen, I wouldn't run away from Luis.

I found him asleep, stretched out on the grass under the shade of the spreading oak at the far end of the garden. He was bare to the waist and wore only denim cutoffs. He was no less sexy with those hypnotic dark eyes closed and I drifted closer and closer, taking care not to rouse him. Finally I eased down at his side, smiling in triumph. Instead of me being the helpless one, he was at my mercy—as long as he didn't wake up.

There was no one to see us—Jed was gone for the day and the hedge blocked any view from the house. Besides, Delia was engrossed in her favorite soap. I leaned over Luis, studying the subtle and enticing contours of his lips before bending down to brush my mouth softly over his. He smiled but didn't rouse.

Greatly daring, I touched the smooth, warm skin of his chest, my forefinger tracing the slender line of dark hair down over his taut, muscled abdomen to the band of his cutoffs. He moaned in his sleep, exciting me. I could do anything I wanted to him and he'd never, never know.

Untying the straps holding up my halter top, I let the cotton fall away from my breasts, baring them. Slowly I leaned over him until my tingling nipples caressed his chest. He whispered a name I thought was mine.

I slipped off my dress and panties. Naked, I undid the snap on the band of his cutoffs and cautiously eased down the zipper, my breath coming faster as I saw he wore nothing underneath. Down and down went the zipper. I could hardly wait until—

I blinked, coming to myself in the library of Bloodstone House, ten years older but no wiser. In my fantasy I'd never gotten those damn shorts off him, probably because I'd never seen Luis completely undressed and my imagination couldn't equal what I was sure must be the thrilling reality.

Caught in my own spell from the past, I leaned over the sleeping Luis until my lips touched his. A moment later I found myself sprawled on top of him, his arms holding me firmly as he kissed me with such heated passion I couldn't have moved even if he'd been willing to let me. So much for fantasy—and to hell with it. Luis, awake and participating, was a wondrous reality beyond anything my imagination could conjure up.

His taste, dark and exotic, added an intoxicating dimension to the kiss. I clung to him as he shifted position so we lay together on the couch, wanting never to be separated from him again.

"Is it a dream?" he whispered against my lips.

"Better than any dream," I murmured, my fingers tangling in his black hair as I gave in to my demanding need to touch him, to caress him, to know all of him.

"I won't let you go this time," he warned, his hand cupping my breast.

I moaned, leaning into his caress, offering myself, wanting him.

Clothes were slipped off and discarded. At some point, I was dimly aware Luis had shut the library door. We lay skin to skin, a delicious and erotic sensation intensified by caresses that set me on fire.

"Luis," I gasped, "please, Luis," catching a glimpse, through half-shut eyes, of his face, taut with passion.

He rose over me and we become one, both of us possessed and possessing as together we found our bliss, moving to earth's eternal rhythm into a final soaring, ecstatic release.

Holding each other afterward as we lay temporarily spent, I told him how I'd fantasized about him when I was a teenager.

"You'll never know how many nights you slept with me," he murmured. "I'd seen you only once in a swimsuit—a maillot, as I recall—but even that hid the salient points so I had to use my imagination." He ran a lazy hand along my hip. "You surpass anything I ever imagined."

"Mmm," I agreed, meaning that I found him magnificent but was too shy to tell him.

"You were always the one I wanted," he said. "Did you realize that back then?"

I shook my head. "I didn't know enough to understand what I wanted, but when you touched me I—well, I melted. I still do."

He smiled, gathering me closer. When he began whispering in my ear about what happened when I touched him, excitement spiraled inside me. I soon discovered that with mere words Luis could take me higher than any other man ever had or would. But those heights were nothing compared to where we flew together.

Enraptured, caught in a web of passion far stronger than my will, I couldn't think of anything except Luis and the magic between us.

Until, as I lay dozing in his arms, I gradually became aware that a sweet scent had drifted into the room. When I recognized the smell I sat up abruptly, looking frantically around. The door was still closed; Luis and I were alone in the library, alone but surrounded by the overpowering scent of lily of the valley.

A strong conviction gripped me, almost as though words were echoing in my mind. Her words. Great-aunt Faith knew exactly what had happened between Luis and me and she didn't approve. Not at all.

CHAPTER NINE

Despite my abrupt movement when I smelled the lily-of-the-valley scent, Luis didn't rouse, though he flung out an arm and began mumbling. Suddenly he said very clearly, "I kept to the bargain. Now it's ended."

I was puzzling over the words he'd spoken in his sleep when his beeper buzzed. Luis blinked once then sprang to his feet in one quick motion and clicked it off. He glanced at me, making me conscious I wore not a stitch of clothing.

"I need a phone," he said, yanking on his shorts and chinos. "I don't recall seeing one."

I reached for my robe and slid into it. "In the entry," I said. "It's sort of hidden in an alcove—I'll show you."

As we left the library, Luis bare to the waist and me clutching my robe together, I hoped the sound of the beeper hadn't awakened the girls or Delia. Especially Delia. Though the girls might not put two and two together, she certainly would.

When I returned to the library, leaving Luis alone with the phone, the lily-of-the-valley scent had dispersed entirely.

Quickly donning my nightgown under the robe, I slid my feet into my slippers and did my best to smooth my hair. Luis returned as the clock struck four.

"I have to go," he said as he dressed. "This kid's got a fever of one hundred and five degrees so I told his parents to bring him to the office and I'd meet them there."

Everything I thought of to say either about what had happened between us or about the sick child sounded incredibly dumb so I kept quiet.

He shoved his feet into his shoes, hooked the beeper on to his belt, looked at me and smiled. "I never did get to that sandwich and coffee, did I?"

I shook my head.

He leaned close and brushed his lips over mine. "I don't want to leave."

Putting an arm around my waist, he drew me with him as he left the library. When we passed the cart, I grabbed four cookies from the plate and handed them to him.

"Four is exactly the right number," he said. "The magic number."

"I thought that was seven."

"Not to my people." At the door he hesitated. "Do you ever wear lily-of-the-valley perfume?"

So he'd smelled it, too. "No," I said. "My great-aunt did, though."

"Yes, I know." He pulled me close, gazing into my eyes. "Be very careful. I'll be back to take Soso home as soon as I get the chance."

I closed and locked the door behind him, bemused by the lingering effects of our lovemaking. I propped the chair under the knob, wondering if I'd behaved like an idiot but still so much under his spell that I didn't really care. "Luis," I whispered, relishing the feel of his name on my tongue.

I climbed the stairs in a daze. When I opened the door to my bedroom, Diablo dashed out and down the stairs, eager, I thought, to reach his food or his sandbox in the storeroom. I drifted across to the connecting room and looked in on the sleeping girls before easing onto my bed, telling myself I'd rest for a few minutes.

Giggling and thuds from the girls' room woke me. I found the sun streaming in my windows and Tibbie and Soso in the midst of a pillow fight.

Luis arrived as we were finishing breakfast but declined to join us other than for coffee.

"I ate at the Thompsonville hospital," he said, "after admitting a patient there early this morning."

Probably the child with the high fever, I thought, gazing at the slightly disheveled Luis and thinking I'd never seen such a sexy man. Delia, setting a cup on the table for Luis, gave me such a sharp glance that I decided I must look like a moonstruck loon and shifted my attention to Soso.

"I really liked having you stay here," I told her, "and I hope you can come again soon."

"Yeah, me too," Tibbie added before Soso had a chance to speak.

Soso stared at her plate. "Thanks," she said shyly. "I had fun."

While she and Tibbie ran upstairs to collect Soso's belongings, I walked through to the entry with Luis.

"I spoke to Grandfather before I came to the house last night," he said. "I meant to tell you sooner but—" he paused, lifting his hand and brushing his forefinger across my lips "—making love with you wiped everything from my mind. It's a wonder I even remember my own name this morning."

I licked his finger and he drew in his breath. Catching me by the shoulders, he said hoarsely, "Don't tempt me. As it is I can barely stop myself from tossing you on the couch and beginning all over again."

My insides turned to liquid at the frustrated passion in both his voice and his expression, making me more than willing to melt into his embrace. With an effort I reminded myself that Tibbie and Soso were apt to appear at any moment.

"What did Running Fox tell you?" I asked, forcing myself not to sway toward him.

Luis dropped his hands and immediately I longed to have him touch me again. "Grandfather said you must give me the four feathers to bring to him. Also he wanted to know what the dream spirit said about the last two feathers."

Dream spirit? Feathers? I gathered my wits. "The third feather was a blue jay's—*Beware a clever thief*. The fourth I don't recognize and I don't recall any message—though I did dream of a closed coffin." I thrust away the memory. "The feathers are upstairs, I'll bring them to you."

The girls clattered past me on the stairs as I went up. Taking an envelope from the writing desk in my bedroom, I inserted the four feathers and glued down the flap. Luis was waiting by the open front door and we walked outside together, joining the girls by his car.

"I'd ask you and Tibbie to come along," he said, "but I have patients to see in the village and in the hills. Then I'll be swinging by the hospital on my way back."

Tibbie's face showed her disappointment; I hoped mine was better concealed. I found my need to be with Luis not only surprising but embarrassing, because I took pride in my hard-earned ability to stand alone, to be the strong one who needed no leaning post.

"I hope to see you tonight," he added, "but I might not be able to. I can't promise."

Tibbie and I watched from the driveway until the car vanished from our sight.

"I miss Soso already," she complained as we walked to the house and sat on the front steps. "I wish we could be sisters. She knows so many neat things about animals and stuff. And we're a lot alike. She doesn't have a father, either, and her birth mother's dead."

"Who does she live with, then?" I asked.

"Her grandma. But her grandma's sick with something Grandfather Running Fox and Luis can't cure and she's going to die pretty soon. After that, Soso might have to go up north to live with some other relatives and she doesn't want to."

I remembered Luis mentioning a grandmother.

"If we stayed here and lived in Bloodstone House all the time," Tibbie went on, "maybe we could ask Soso to come and live with us after her grandma dies."

"But we're not staying here," I reminded her gently, feeling sorry for Soso.

She sighed. "Yeah, I know. But I wish we could."

Hearing a car pulling into the circular driveway, I rose and Tibbie got up, too, as Travis's shiny red sports car pulled up in front of the steps.

"That's really like wow," Tibbie said to him, watching him climb from the car.

"A girl after my own heart," Travis said, putting a hand on her shoulder. "*Wow* is the perfect word."

The three of us entered the house together. I invited Travis to have coffee with me while Tibbie trailed into the music room to practice the piano.

Travis sat across from me at the glass-topped table in the morning room, remaining silent as he stirred and stirred his coffee until I was ready to dump it in his lap. Stubbornly I decided I was damned if I'd speak first.

"Since it appears you, Tibbie, and Delia are all healthy," he said finally, "you didn't need a doctor last night. Therefore, I assume you must believe Luis more capable of standing off an intruder than I am."

I blinked. So he knew Luis had been here. Since I'm chronically unable to abide by the advice to never apologize and never explain, I said, "It's true Luis came by this morning to pick up Soso."

"Came by?" Travis raised his eyebrows. "When did he leave?"

Was he trying to make me feel guilty? Annoyance seeped into my voice. "I didn't realize you took such an interest in who came and went from Bloodstone House."

"Under ordinary circumstances, obviously I wouldn't. But yesterday you gave me the impression you felt the house was under siege and you needed a knight errant. Foolishly enough, I thought you'd chosen me for the role." What sounded like genuine hurt tinged his words. "Yet you turned me away and chose Luis instead."

"It wasn't like that at all. Jed's truck broke down in Visalia so he wasn't able to get back with the dead bolts. In fact, he hasn't returned yet. Luis arrived after Jed called me with the bad news and offered—well, actually what you'd offered. Without the bolts in place, I felt vulnerable so I asked him to stay. Really, Travis, I resent being put through a third degree.''

He sighed. ''Sorry. I rode over on horseback after midnight, planning to camp on your grounds and keep watch from the outside since you refused to let me stay inside. When I saw Luis's four-wheel parked in the driveway I waited until it became clear he wasn't going to leave. Figuring you didn't need me, I rode home.'' He gave me a sheepish grin. ''I'll admit I was a tad peeved.''

His explanation canceled my irritation with him. How could I stay angry when Travis's only intention was to protect me?

''Old Luis has always been formidable competition,'' Travis said. ''All the more so now that he's a doctor, not some penniless Indian from the hills.''

''I don't choose friends by their position or how much money they have,'' I said indignantly.

Travis lifted his hands, palms up. ''I seem to have a talent for saying the wrong thing to you this morning. The truth is I have nothing but admiration for Luis's accomplishments. Though it was a generous gesture on your great-aunt's part to give Luis the money to go to college and and med school, I must say no one deserved it more than he.''

I was so taken aback I couldn't speak. Great-aunt Faith had put Luis through med school? When she was noted for her tightfistedness with money and had never seemed to like Luis?

Apparently noting my surprise, Travis said, ''I thought you knew.''

I shook my head. ''Why did she do it?'' I asked.

He shrugged. ''My mother figured it was the only way Miss Faith could be certain of having a doctor at her beck and call. Naranada isn't exactly a physician's mecca."

That was true. As far as I knew the town had never had a doctor until Luis set up practice. Still, college and med school were expensive and a gift of such a large sum of money was not only atypical of my great-aunt, it was almost unbelievable.

"She must have loaned Luis the money," I said more to myself than to Travis.

"No. I understand she gave him an outright gift."

While I was wondering why neither my great-aunt nor Luis had ever mentioned this to me, Travis changed the subject.

"I've set the night for my party," he said. "Next Sunday. Okay?"

About to nod agreement, I paused to count days. "But that's my birthday."

"I know. What better reason for a party? And Tibbie's invited, too. I wouldn't leave her out of her mother's birthday celebration."

"I don't know, Travis," I said slowly, recalling all too clearly what had happened the last time I celebrated my birthday in Naranada and the part Travis had played.

"You mean you don't want a birthday party?" Travis's gaze traveled past me. "What do you think, Tibbie?"

I turned to see Tibbie standing in the doorway.

"I heard you say I was invited," she told Travis. "Thanks." Looking at me, she added, "I think it's a neat idea, Mom."

Since I was reluctant to mention, in front of Tibbie, the reason I hesitated, I merely said, "I'll think about it."

"That usually means yes," Tibbie confided to Travis, "but not always. I like parties but Mom doesn't go to very many so maybe she doesn't."

"Come on, Val, it'll be fun," Travis urged. "I promise you'll have the time of your life."

Why not? I asked myself. Saying no would disappoint Tibbie and, after all, what danger could there be in going to Travis's house for a party?

"I see I'm outnumbered," I said. "All right, then, but please, no birthday presents."

"I'll mention that to the guests but I'm pretending I didn't hear you."

"Travis, I really don't want any gifts."

"Never deny the giver the joy of giving. That's from the Bible, so don't argue."

I smiled, conceding the point, aware that Travis would do exactly as he wanted no matter how much I protested.

Shortly after, Jed arrived and Travis insisted on helping him install the dead bolts. While they were working, Tibbie and I went to the corral with sugar for Misty, then fed the ducks in the pond. When the bread crumbs were gone, we sat on the bench beside the pond under the shade of a weeping willow, watching the three ducks swim away from us.

"Soso said we should get one more duck," Tibbie said.

"Because four is the Miwok's magic number?"

"You heard that from Luis, right?"

I nodded.

"I told Soso about my spells," Tibbie said after a few moments. "I was afraid once she knew she might think I was too weird to be friends with, the way some of the kids back in Santa Cruz felt, but I figured she ought to know. Anyway, what she said was once I found what the spirit was looking for it would stop bothering me and go away and then I wouldn't have any more spells. Do you think maybe she's right?''

The hopeful look on Tibbie's face made me choose my words carefully. "I guess we'll have to wait and see." Not that I believed Soso knew what she was talking about, but what she'd said made as much sense as what some of the doctors had told me.

"Soso's seen lots more kinds of owls besides the white one that lives near our house," Tibbie went on. "She says after bad people die, sometimes their spirits go into owls."

Again I trod with care. "Her people have different beliefs from ours."

"Yeah, I know. But I got to wondering. Maybe she's right and we're wrong—how can you be sure?"

"I don't know the answer—maybe none of us is right."

Tibbie thought that one over for some time. "Just in case, though," she asked finally, "can we get another duck?"

"Did I hear you say you're looking for another duck?" Travis asked from behind us. "Three aren't enough?"

"Four would be better," Tibbie said.

"I'm sure we have a spare duck among the fowl population at my ranch. I'll bring one over."

Tibbie smiled at him. "That's great, Mr. York. Thanks."

"I'm always delighted to oblige pretty girls."

Tibbie, not accustomed to teasing flattery, glanced at me uncertainly.

"Have you and Jed finished with the bolts?" I asked Travis.

"He was putting the last one on when I left."

"The least I can do in return for your help is to offer you lunch."

"Thanks, no. I may drop by later in the day, though."

"With the duck?" Tibbie asked.

He grinned at her. "Beware of Greeks bearing gifts, Helen. See you later."

When he was out of earshot, Tibbie asked, "Why did he call me Helen?"

"Are you ready to listen to a long story?"

She rolled her eyes. "I guess."

I told her about beautiful Helen and how Paris had stolen her from her home in Sparta and brought her to his walled city-state of Troy. I skipped quickly through the angry Greeks setting sail for Troy to free Helen and the many battles fought once they arrived, because I wanted to get to the horse itself.

"So after a handful of Greek soldiers secretly climbed into the giant wooden horse on wheels that they'd built, the rest of their army pretended to sail away," I said. "Though warned by one of the priests to fear Greeks even when they bear gifts, the Trojans pulled the horse through the gates into their walled city, never dreaming what was inside it.

"That night, the Greek soldiers crept from the belly of the horse and opened the locked gates to let in the rest of their army. And so Troy was destroyed, the men were killed and, except for Helen, who went back home, its women were sold into slavery."

Tibbie grimaced. "Ugh, how awful. But why did Mr. York say it to me? Did he mean I'm supposed to beware of someone trying to give me something that looks like a gift?''

"Travis meant to be amusing," I said, smiling. "I think we can accept the duck he promised without worrying about being destroyed or sold into slavery."

Tibbie remained thoughtful on the way to the house. In the entry she examined herself in the gilt-framed mirror, turning her head this way and that.

"Nope," she said at last. "I look sort of okay, I guess, but I'm not pretty. Or beautiful, like Helen in the story."

"Don't take what Travis says literally," I told her. "He likes to tease. And, if you want my opinion, you're far and away the most okay-looking nine-year-old girl in Naranada."

Tibbie giggled. "You're being silly again, Mom."

After lunch I found myself scarcely able to keep my eyes open, so, leaving Tibbie with Delia, I took a nap. It was late afternoon when I woke to the wonderful smell of yeast bread baking.

"Delia and I made rolls," Tibbie informed me when I came into the kitchen. "You get to taste them at supper."

After eating early, Tibbie, Delia and I played several games of hearts—I won one—and I was almost able to feel that everything was normal and all was well. Except that every time the new bolt on the kitchen door caught my eye, I was reminded of why I'd had it put there.

Travis returned at dusk. "Your new duck is in the pond with the others," he told Tibbie. "They seem to like her. Or him. With white ducks it's hard to tell which is which."

She wanted to go and look and so we did, for a few minutes, watching the four ducks drift lazily. As we were returning to the house, I glanced involuntarily at Mount Sangre and held for an instant, thinking I'd seen a flash of light at the top. When it didn't come again, I decided to say nothing to Travis.

"Is the party you're having for my mom a night-time party?" Tibbie asked him.

"I'd planned an evening party, yes."

"Good. 'Cause I hardly ever get to stay up late."

"You'll get to stay late at my party—I guarantee it."

Tibbie shot me a triumphant glance and I shrugged. It wouldn't hurt her to be up late one night. Her spells probably had made me overprotective of her.

Back at the house we played hearts again—Travis and Tibbie and I—but after the second game I began to yawn.

"I think your mother is trying to tell me something," Travis said to Tibbie as I smothered yet another yawn.

"Sorry," I said. "I'm afraid this will have to be an early night for me."

"I know a hint when I'm hit over the head with one," Travis said. "Just let me take a last glance at the windows to make sure everything's locked and then I'm outa here."

I bolted the door behind Travis, feeling much more secure with the extra locks in place, secure enough not to sit up all night. We'd be safe; I could go to bed.

"Can I—I mean, may I bring Diablo to my room?" Tibbie asked. "He behaves himself really well."

I debated, finally deciding that the kitten wouldn't be likely to stay in her bed all night anyway—he hadn't the night before—so why not give her the comfort of going to sleep with him? No doubt my reluctance to let her take the kitten to bed with her came from my great-aunt's refusal to allow Sombra to sleep with me.

"Cats, even one as clean as Sombra, carry germs," she'd insisted, giving me a list of the various nasty diseases I could expect to come down with if Sombra spent the night in my bed. My great-aunt, I realized now, must have spent each summer worrying about what might happen to me.

I wouldn't allow myself to become like her, I vowed. Though I needed to watch over Tibbie, I wouldn't worry excessively over every little thing that might affect her.

"All right," I said, "Diablo can sleep with you. I'll leave my door open a crack so he can go downstairs if he needs to."

She rewarded me with a happy grin before scooping Diablo into her arms.

Once Tibbie and the cat were snuggled together in her bed, I found I wasn't as sleepy as I'd been earlier. Thinking I'd read, I glanced at my nightstand and saw only the thin volume of poems Luis had given me. If I'd been in Santa Cruz reading them, I'd have enjoyed the poems. Here at Bloodstone House, though, I found Webb's imagery unsettling. Especially at night.

There'd been so much talk of ghosts walking and spirits influencing the living that my grip on reality felt threatened.

Did I want to bother going down to the library to choose something else? While I tried to make up my mind, I crossed to the window and looked into the night. Though I couldn't see Mount Sangre from my room, I was reminded of the light I'd thought I'd seen at the top and remembered this was the second time. I wished I'd mentioned it to Travis.

Were there lights up there now? I knew I'd be unable to rest until I took a look at the hill. That meant going downstairs for a decent view of Mount Sangre. Glancing into Tibbie's room, I saw she was already asleep. Not bothering with a robe or slippers, I padded into the hall and down the stairs.

Though I'd left far fewer lights on than I had the night before, one of the sconces in the entry was lit, enabling me to find my way without difficulty. The best view, I knew, was from the front steps, but I hesitated to unlock the door, peering instead through the long and narrow window on the right side of the door.

A light at the top! Flickering rather than steady. What could it be? Who was up there and what were they doing? I longed for a better look. Turning on the outside light, I scanned the steps and what I could see of the yard beyond. There was no one in sight.

Taking a deep breath, I shut off the light, unlocked and opened the front door and stepped cautiously outside.

As I stared up at Mount Sangre, I heard a faint chanting. From the top? I listened and was sure of it. Though the July night was warm, I hugged myself against an inner chill. There was no doubt in my mind the chanting and the flickering light were connected. Reminded of the black candle and the invocation ten years ago, I tasted fear on my tongue.

What dreadful ceremony was being enacted on that bloody hill this night?

CHAPTER TEN

Alarmed by the lights and sounds at the top of Mount Sangre, I fled into the house, locking and bolting the door behind me. As I hugged myself, trembling, I tried in vain to convince myself that nothing more dangerous than local pranksters chanted as they waved flaming torches. How could I believe such a simple explanation when I'd felt skin-prickling waves of power flowing down from the top of the hill?

Power might not be the right word, but I'd definitely felt something being generated by the flames and the chants, something that had tingled through me, raising the hair on my neck and setting my teeth on edge.

I didn't feel it now. Perhaps the house was a barrier. Or maybe my imagination was more active than I'd ever suspected and I'd frightened myself into feeling a force that didn't exist.

The lights were real enough. And I'd heard voices, not merely one voice chanting. Strangers had invaded Mount Sangre this night for God only knows what purpose. I had no intention of trying to discover who they were or why they were there, at least not until morning. Even in broad daylight I wasn't sure I could bring myself to climb to the top.

I took a deep breath and let it out slowly. I was safe inside the house and so was Tibbie. The doors were bolted shut, the windows locked. No one could get inside without breaking in and that would make enough noise to give me a chance to call for help.

I walked slowly into the library where a desk light cast a dim glow, creating sinister shadows that seemed to make the carved griffins framing the fireplace snarl at me. Should I sit up in here? I moved my shoulders uneasily. What if Tibbie had one of her spells and wandered away? I'd never hear her if she went down the back stairs. Soso had been with her the night before but Soso was gone. Either I must return to my room or else wake Tibbie and bring her to the library with me.

After some thought, I lifted the poker from the hearth set and carried it up the stairs with me as a weapon of sorts, should I need one.

Tibbie slept restlessly. While I watched her, Diablo leaped off her bed and trotted from the room. Deserting us. I shook my head at such a morbid thought. The little cat had needs of his own that had nothing to do with Tibbie and me. Love for my daughter swelled my heart as I gazed at her. I'd come back to Bloodstone House with the hope she'd improve here. Had it been a wise decision?

Tibbie loved being here, she adored Misty, liked country living and found the old house fascinating. She'd even made a new friend. If I suggested we leave tomorrow I'd face a storm of protest. She'd be a long time forgiving me and might not understand for years, if ever, why I forced her to leave a place where she was happy when I'd promised we'd stay until school started.

I'd do anything to keep her safe, including tolerating her disappointment and disapproval. But was she really in danger? Luis seemed to think she might be, though I didn't understand why. If I were to believe in the dream warnings, I'd say they were directed at me, not Tibbie.

And the intruder? Was I reading too much into the incident? Where in the world *could* you be safe from would-be thieves? On two different occasions in Santa Cruz we'd had prowlers attempt to break into our apartment and fail. The police had caught the last one—a teenage boy on drugs.

I hated to leave Luis just as much as Tibbie would hate to leave Bloodstone House. Still, to be on the safe side, we ought to go sooner than September so I'd best begin preparing her for an earlier departure. Not tomorrow, but next week. After Travis's party, because Tibbie was eagerly looking forward to that.

When at last I propped myself up on my pillows, the poker within easy reach, my gloomy thoughts had succeeded in undermining my shaky confidence, making me feel as though I might never dare to sleep again.

Luis, I thought, why aren't you here? Remembering his caresses, I relaxed against the pillows and sighed, losing myself in a pleasant reverie until I heard a board creak somewhere downstairs.

I sat bolt upright, gripping the poker and listening, but the sound wasn't repeated. Reminding myself that the old house was full of creaks and groans, I eased back against the pillows, keeping my hand on the poker, tense and alert.

Despite my fear, sometime later I must have dozed, because I woke with a start, my heart pounding. Tibbie stood in her doorway, outlined by the night-light in her room.

I had to swallow before I could speak. "What's wrong, Tibbie?" I asked, the words sticking in my throat because I was afraid I knew.

"Where is he?" she said plaintively as she walked into my room, her eyes fixed on nothing as they always were during her spells. She would have continued on past my bed to the door if I hadn't jumped up and grasped her arm.

"Come into my bed," I said, pulling her gently toward me.

She resisted, struggling against me, and I stared at her in surprise. Never before in a spell had she fought me.

Since I was bigger and stronger, I could have forced her into my bed and held her there but I didn't want to hurt her. Making a quick decision, I let her go, retaining a grip on her hand, and said, "All right, I'll go with you." I grabbed the poker with my free hand.

Tibbie led me into the hall and down the steps. The sconce was still lit in the entry, and, for a long moment, she stood at the foot of the stairs as though listening.

I listened, too. Very faint and far away, something wailed, making my nape prickle. Did the sound come from outside?

Tibbie turned toward the library. With me beside her, she crossed to the closed door—had I closed it? I couldn't recall. Unease gripped me. When she put her hand on the knob, the wailing came again. Definitely from somewhere inside the house. Inside the library. Tibbie opened the door.

The lit desk lamp cast insufficient light, so I let go of Tibbie to flick on the wall switch. As I did, Tibbie ran to the fireplace. When I reached her she was tracing a griffin with her fingers as though trying to memorize the carving. She felt the two griffins to the right, then the two to the left, pausing at the last.

I blinked when I saw her grasp and twist the griffin. The head turned under her fingers and, to my amazement, the wood paneling below the griffin swung open. Something dark leaped out. I gasped, lunging backward and pulling Tibbie with me. I lost the poker as we sprawled onto the floor.

Tibbie sat up first, putting her hand to her head. "Diablo?" she said. "Where's Diablo?"

I saw the kitten's white mask peer from under the couch and belatedly realized it must have been Diablo I'd heard wailing, Diablo I'd seen freed from the secret compartment in the paneling. Only then did I remember what Tibbie had said when she first went into the spell. Not the usual "Where is it?" but "Where is he?"

She'd been searching for Diablo and she'd found him.

Tibbie coaxed the kitten from under the couch and held him close, petting him. Only when she was convinced he was all right did she look around the room and then at me.

"Did I have a spell?" she asked.

"Not exactly but something like one, I guess." I gestured toward the opening that was scarcely large enough to contain the kitten. "You freed Diablo from there."

"I knew I heard something," Delia said, standing in the doorway in her robe and slippers. "What's happened now?"

"Look," I said to her. "Did you know there was a secret panel by the fireplace?"

Delia shook her head, coming closer. "Land o' Goshen, what next?"

All three of us examined the secret compartment. I reached inside. At first I thought it was empty, but then I felt softness under my fingers and picked it up. We all stared at the four feathers in my hand.

"The owl was in there, too," Tibbie said suddenly, "but now he's gone."

"What owl?" I asked. "How do you know?"

"Why, it's plain as the bristles on a hog that we've found Miss Faith's hidey-hole," Delia said.

The owl medallion! But if my great-aunt had hidden anything in this secret place, it was gone now.

"How do you know about the owl?" I asked Tibbie again.

"I don't know, I just do. The same way I knew I had to find Diablo." She fondled the kitten's ears.

I had no idea what it meant, but she'd never before recalled anything that had happened during a spell.

"Who put my cat in that awful place?" Tibbie demanded.

"You mean the kitten was in the hidey-hole?" Delia said. "Well, I never!"

"He must have crawled in through the fireplace," I insisted, not wanting to believe Diablo had been put there. Transferring the feathers to my left hand, I felt around inside the compartment again but could find no other openings.

"Mom, you saw for yourself Diablo wouldn't come in the library while the owl was inside that hiding place," Tibbie said. "He knew it was here and it scared him. The person who took the owl put Diablo in there after he made Diablo find the owl for him."

I was trying to make sense of this when I heard Delia draw in her breath.

"Look, Miss Valora." She pointed.

I saw lacy leaves crumbled on the floor by the closed draperies, leaves from the wisteria that climbed the wall outside the library. Striding to the window, I flung open the draperies. The window was closed but unlocked. Even as I locked it, I understood it not only was too late but not necessary. The intruder had found what he came for—the owl medallion—and he wouldn't be back.

"He's gone, isn't he?" Tibbie asked.

I nodded. We hadn't searched the house to make certain but I was sure I was right. Opening my left hand, I examined the feathers. Hummingbird, redwinged blackbird, blue jay, and the unknown spotted feather—the same four I'd dreamed of and found in my room. The feathers, I thought, smelled faintly of lilies of the valley.

"Delia," I said, confused and fearful, "I don't understand what's going on."

"To my way of thinking, Miss Faith's ghost has been trying to tell us someone was after what was inside her hidey-hole. In her last months Miss Faith must have forgot she'd put it there and that's why she was searching for it. She might have been forgetful when she was alive, but her ghost wouldn't be. Ghosts know everything."

Delia's words failed to comfort me.

"The prowler's gone and we're none of us hurt," she pointed out. "That's something to be thankful for. What I think is we could all use some hot cocoa right about now."

I was about to agree when I was startled by the banging of the front door knocker. Tibbie reached for my hand.

"Mercy!" Delia exclaimed. "Who can it be at this hour?"

I retrieved the dropped poker and nudged Tibbie toward Delia. "I'll go see. You two stay here."

The banging continued. Turning on the outside light, I peered anxiously through the side window, hoping against hope I'd see Luis.

But it was Travis, instead—also a welcome sight. I unlocked and opened the door.

"I lost the bastard," he said as he entered. "Took after him but he had too much of a head start. You all right?"

"I'm not hurt, if that's what you mean, but I'm decidedly not all right." I struggled not to burst into tears for fear of frightening Tibbie. "Do you mean you were chasing the thief?"

As Travis nodded, I saw Delia and Tibbie peering cautiously around the open library door. Diablo squirmed free of Tibbie's arms and dashed toward the kitchen.

"Why it's Mr. York," Delia said. "Come along to the kitchen with me, Tibbie, you can help make the cocoa."

"We'll all go there," I said, longing for the safety and comfort I used to find in the kitchen when I was younger.

"Go ahead," Travis said. "I'll join you as soon as I've checked that window the prowler used. I'm sure it was locked earlier."

Tibbie and I were setting the table when Travis ambled into the kitchen and perched on a stool. "Loose window latch,'' he said. ''I fixed it temporarily—get Jed to look at it later.''

I nodded. ''You didn't tell me you intended to provide guard duty every night.''

Travis shrugged. ''What are friends for? I rode over on horseback again—unfortunately later than I'd intended. I'd no more than tied Ajax to a post and unrolled my sleeping bag under an oak when I noticed one of the library windows looked as if it was open. I started over to investigate when a dark figure climbed from the open window, shut it quickly and was turning away when he saw me running toward him.

''He took off like a bat out of hell. If I'd been on Ajax I could have ridden him down but as it was—'' Travis shrugged. ''When he ducked into the shadows of the tangerine grove I couldn't see him any longer and he got away. Is anything missing?''

''I think he took something of my great-aunt's, but I'm not sure.''

I half expected Tibbie to chime in, saying she knew exactly what the thief had stolen and that he'd also imprisoned her cat, but she remained silent, her solemn gaze shifting from Travis to me and back again. At the stove, her back to us, Delia stirred the hot milk and cocoa in silence.

''Anything valuable?'' Travis asked.

''I'm not sure,'' I repeated. It wasn't that I didn't trust Travis, for I did, but I couldn't bring myself to mention the owl medallion to him.

''I'm glad no one was hurt,'' Travis said. ''I retrieved Ajax and rode up and down searching for the bastard. Didn't find a sign. I never did get a good look at him, worse luck. You didn't happen to see him, did you? If we can give our local cop a description—''

"He was gone by the time we came downstairs. And I don't see any need to call in the police. What can Naranada's one-man force do? The thief's gone and he won't be back."

Travis frowned. "He won't be back? That's an odd comment."

Delia scuffed over to pour hot cocoa into our cups while Tibbie, behind her, popped a marshmallow on top.

"Want me to make toast?" Delia asked.

"Yes, please," I said.

"I'll get the jelly and peanut butter," Tibbie offered.

"Why don't you think the thief will return?" Travis persisted.

I'd tried to avoid answering because I didn't want to discuss the medallion. "There's no need." My voice was clipped. "This wasn't an ordinary thief, this was one who knew exactly what he wanted, found it and took it."

Travis sipped his cocoa in silence, obviously thinking over what I'd said. He accepted a slice of buttered toast from the plate Delia passed, absently spreading it with orange marmalade.

"Stop puttering and sit down with us," I told Delia.

Wordlessly she obeyed. Tibbie glanced around the table but didn't speak. Faint bongs from the entry clock reminded me it was four in the morning. We all ought to be in bed.

Finally Travis finished the last bite of toast and looked at me. "Did I mention that after I lost track of the thief I heard one of those big bikes rev up and take off?" he asked.

A motorcycle! I thought immediately of Willa's long-ago boyfriend. Was it possible Jack Norton had come back to Naranada after all these years? Willa had certainly been with him after that night on Mount Sangre and, though she didn't remember what had happened to her after the storm began, it was entirely possible she'd told him about the first part of the evening. About the book of incantations and the owl medallion.

"If Jack *was* the thief," I said aloud, speaking to myself as much as to anyone else, "why would he want the medallion?"

"I thought so," Travis said triumphantly.

"You mean about Jack?"

"No, that it was the owl medallion the thief took. Why the hell wouldn't you say so?"

"Never mind—what about Jack Norton?"

Travis shrugged. "All we have to go on is the sound of a motorcycle. I can't even connect it directly to the man I chased."

I shivered, imagining a vindictive Jack blaming me for what had happened to Willa. He could still have ties in Naranada—had he heard I was staying at Bloodstone House with Willa's child? His child, despite both his and Willa's disclaimers?

Even though the idea frightened me, in a way I hoped it was true. If Jack had been the one who'd raped Willa, then neither Luis nor Travis was guilty. I'd far rather it had been a stranger than someone I knew and wanted to trust.

But what could Jack be up to now? How did he plan to use the medallion? And how could he have possibly known where it was hidden?

Of course, Willa could have discovered my great-aunt's hiding place years ago and told Jack about it. What else might Willa have said to him that he could use against us?

I put a protective arm around Tibbie. He needn't think he had any right to so much as speak to her!

"Don't look so upset," Travis said. "I'll stand guard outside until daylight."

"Who's Jack Norton?" Tibbie asked.

"Someone who used to live in town," I temporized. "If you've finished your cocoa and toast, it's past time you got back to bed. Me, too."

Letting Travis out the kitchen door, I thanked him for his help. "You've been a friend indeed," I said.

He smiled at me. "It's a step in the right direction, I guess."

Not until Tibbie and I were climbing the back stairs did I realize she was carrying Diablo once again. "I didn't see him in the kitchen—where did he come from?" I asked.

"He was hiding in his room."

I nodded. The storeroom off the kitchen.

"I think maybe he doesn't like Mr. York," she said.

"You can't blame him if he doesn't trust people he doesn't know well—not after being shut into that secret compartment."

"Yeah. That'd be scary." She didn't say any more until we entered my room. As we came to my bed, she paused. "Mom, would it be okay if Diablo and I slept with you for the rest of the night?" she asked.

"You're welcome, but I'll have to see how Diablo behaves."

"He'll stay on my side of the bed."

After we were lying side by side with the kitten curled next to her, she said, "Is the robber really not ever going to come back?"

"I don't think he will. That window latch was loose and he must have jiggled the window until the latch popped open. Jed will make certain all the latches are secure, just as a precaution."

"It's scary when bad people get into your house."

"Yes." I longed to promise her nothing bad would ever come near her again, but I always tried to tell her the truth so I gave her what reassurance I could. "I'll do all I can to make sure it doesn't happen again."

"You looked kind of funny carrying that poker when you answered the door, Mom."

"I can imagine."

She sighed. "I wish Soso could come and stay with me again soon."

"I hope she can," I said, feeling guilty because I doubted there'd be time if I left next week, as I planned.

"Did you know her people have lots of different names for the same thing? I wrote some of them down—like for coyote. Sometimes he's *aheli* and sometimes *woto* and—"

"Isn't 'Coyote' what she called Travis?"

"Yeah. *Yutu*. I asked her why she picked that one 'cause *aheli* sounds better and she told me the different names mean what the coyote is doing. Like *wootci* means coyote barking. She said *yutu* was the name that came into her head."

"What exactly does *yutu* mean?"

"Coyote pretending not to notice prey."

"Travis?" I chuckled. "I'd have called him *wootci*."

It was as comforting for me to have Tibbie in my bed as it was for her to be there. Neither of us woke until nearly noon when Lucy Jennings knocked on my door.

"Delia said I better come up and tell you Dr. Redhawk's here," she said.

Luis was in the library, examining the open compartment in the griffin paneling when I came in.

"Sorry to wake you up," he said.

"I slept enough. I suppose Delia told you about our thief."

"I didn't finish at the hospital until after midnight—I wish to hell I'd come anyway, late as it was. My being here would have prevented this. What was taken from here? Delia neglected to mention it."

"The owl medallion," I said.

Luis scowled. "That's what I was afraid of."

"I think the thief might have been Jack Norton."

"Norton? That biker Willa used to hang out with? He's been gone for years. I hadn't heard he was back in town."

For Luis's benefit I rehashed the night from beginning to end, my account and Travis's mixed together. "So it could have been Jack," I finished.

"Let me think about it," he said. "You haven't had breakfast. Mind if I join you? We can talk later."

After we ate, Luis and I walked Tibbie to the corral where Jed promised to watch her ride Misty. I asked Jed to check all the window latches when Tibbie was through.

On the way back to the house, I mentioned what Tibbie had said about Soso's grandmother, adding, "Is it true Soso may have to leave the Miwok village?"

"Old Mary Quail is dying of liver cancer. When she does, I plan to bring Soso to live in town with me, though I haven't yet told her."

"It's wonderful of you to take her in, but you really ought to share your plans with Soso. She's worried about being sent somewhere up north."

He nodded. "I'll do that."

I was thinking about Luis's generosity and wondering if he'd regret it when he came face-to-face with the responsibilities involved in raising a child, when a glimpse of Mount Sangre reminded me of what I'd seen the night before. Pausing, I stared at the top of the hill, reliving the fright.

"What's the matter?" Luis asked, putting his arm around my shoulders.

"I didn't connect the two until now," I said, "but before the thief came through the library window, there was some kind of—of ceremony on Mount Sangre. Torches. Chanting. I'd planned to look into it today but—"

"I've got time. We'll do it now. Come on." He grasped my hand.

I resisted. "Luis, no. I don't think I can."

"Why?"

Ashamed to admit my fear, I looked anywhere but at him. "I might not to be able to."

He turned my face so I was forced to gaze directly into his eyes. "You don't mean physically, do you?"

I jerked free. "I do mean physically. I tried to climb it when I saw Tibbie with you on that damned hill and I couldn't make myself."

"You'll be able to with me." He spoke confidently. "Together we can do anything."

I almost believed him. Until we reached the foot of Mount Sangre, where I halted abruptly. "No, I can't," I said, panic threatening.

"Close your eyes."

I obeyed.

"Imagine yourself walking up the path to the gazebo," he said softly. "The path is long and the steps steep, but the gazebo is your goal and what awaits you there makes the climb worthwhile. Hold my hand and don't open your eyes until I tell you. Keep the image of the gazebo before you, the gazebo and your reward when you reach it."

I wondered if Luis could possibly know that as a teenager I'd always imagined my dream lover awaited me in the gazebo. I wondered if he had any idea that somehow the dream lover had acquired his face, his body and it was his kiss, his embrace I began to dream of, no longer a nameless fantasy.

"The path is long," Luis repeated, his hand firmly holding mine. "The path is hard. But I'm with you."

Eyes shut, I moved forward with him, bemused by his cadenced words, "We walk together along the steep path, always together. The wind cannot blow us away, the wind cannot throw us away. We are protected. We are guarded. The spirit of the south watches over us, his cloak of feathers holds back the darkness, the darkness beyond the edge of the world. He dances for us, he dances away the evil that reaches with dark spider fingers, the evil that slithers snake-like.

"*Kuksu* dances away the evil with his raven cloak, with his hawk wings, he blows away the darkness with his eagle whistle. In the whirlwind of his dance, the poison of evil Hamaua, Grandfather of rattlesnakes, is flung far and far, the poison is scattered among the fire trails of the stars. Kuksu watches over us. We are safe, we are protected.''

Luis slipped into the tongue of his people, the unknown words falling softly around me, caressing me like the fluff of feathers. A part of me knew I was climbing but it didn't upset me. I felt nothing bad could happen within the protective cocoon of words Luis fashioned around us.

When at last we came to a halt, his chant stopped, too.

"Open your eyes, Valora," he told me.

I obeyed, blinking in the bright sunlight, unable for a moment to see clearly. When I could, I found myself looking down at Bloodstone House and the Rolland groves and acres. I was on top of Mount Sangre, the last place in the world I wanted to be.

"Turn around," Luis said.

Slowly, reluctantly, I turned and faced the massive gray-and-black stone with its flattened top, the stone Travis had used for an obscene altar ten years ago.

Now there was no candle, no circle of blood. But I drew in my breath when I saw a white owl feather in the center of the rock. Next to it, the quills pointed toward each other as though ready to duel, lay a shiny black feather.

I licked dry lips, striving to calm myself, staring from its glistening blackness to the pristine white of the snowy owl feather. Seemingly innocent feathers, yet they terrified me.

CHAPTER ELEVEN

I stood where I'd hoped never to be again, at the top of Mount Sangre, staring at the feathers on the rock. "Somebody *was* on this hill last night!" I cried. "What does it mean?"

Luis took my arm, turning me away from the rock. Below I could see the York ranch house and acreage, reminding me how Mount Sangre separated my property from Travis's. I couldn't understand why the early Yorks and Rollands had argued over possession of Mount Sangre—who'd want it?

I grew conscious of perspiration beading my forehead. Exposed as we were at the very top of the hill, with no shade, the sun's heat was almost unbearable. Yet what unnerved me wasn't the heat but something more intangible, an unseen menace that set my teeth on edge. Evidently Luis felt uncomfortable, too, because he grasped my hand and started down the hill, pulling me with him.

"Don't worry about what you saw up here the night before," he said.

"Why shouldn't I worry? Nothing good ever happens on Mount Sangre."

"This was different. Grandfather believes he's been warned of danger so he sent messages to other Miwok clans. I was too busy to participate but the *Kuksuyu* dancers must have answered his summons."

"Kuksuyu?" I repeated, recalling how he'd called on something named Kuksu to guard us as we climbed Mount Sangre.

"They're feather dancers representing Kuksu, the Spirit of the South, the only spirit strong enough to overcome Hamaua, a shapeshifter who represents evil. The black feather comes from one of their cloaks made of raven feathers."

"And the owl feather?"

"It means that evil, in the form of a white owl, challenges Kuksu. What you saw and heard were Miwok Kuksuyu dancers trying to banish the evil hidden in the stone." He shook his head. "The position of the two feathers means they failed."

Luis was more deeply involved in the customs and rituals of his people than I had realized and it disturbed me. "I've had enough of evil omens and of feathers," I cried. "I wish I'd never returned to Naranada."

Luis didn't speak again until we reached the bottom of the hill. "I agree there's danger for you here and that troubles me. But I can't be sorry you came back to me." He stopped, swung me into his arms and kissed me and, for as long as it lasted, his kiss canceled everything else.

Even after he let me go, the magic of his embrace lingered to lighten my heart.

"I know you're upset," he said as we walked on hand in hand, "and you've reason to be. Grandfather sent the message to the Kuksuyu dancers because of the warning he saw in your four feathers. The fourth feather, he says, was from a mourning dove."

I might have guessed, I thought, if I'd connected the coffin in my dream with the feather. I didn't want to hear what Running Fox found in the feathers and yet I feared not to.

"How did he read the feathers?" I asked.

"You provided clues and so did I. The hummingbird prefers red flowers, his feather means blood. The red-winged blackbird, as I told Grandfather, carries the deadly organism causing equine encephalitis, often fatal to or disabling to humans—darkness within, in other words. The blue jay is a thief and the mourning dove signifies death. Grandfather put it this way— 'Beware the thief who carries darkness within him, for his coming brings darkness and death.'"

A shiver ran through me despite the heat. "A thief did come," I said slowly. "He stole the owl medallion." A thought struck me. "I forgot to tell you I found four more feathers, the same as the others, in that secret compartment." Recalling the lily-of-the-valley scent, I added, "I don't believe the thief put them there."

"No, he wouldn't have. They were left for you as a second warning by Miss Faith."

I stared at him. "Delia insists her ghost is walking through the house at night. Don't tell me you think so, too."

Luis shrugged. "Let's say I don't disbelieve. I've learned there are unseen forces in the world beyond the natural ones such as the wind, earthquakes and so on. Many call these spirits or ghosts. The shamans among my people have, since ancient times, interacted with a few of these forces. I don't know what they are, but I know they exist and I know the force embedded in the rock atop Mount Sangre is powerful and evil.

"For centuries the Miwoks have been aware of the danger on Mount Sangre. Long before the Californios or the Americanos came here, Grandfather says, Kuksu himself taught my people a ceremony to be performed each summer, a Kuksuyu dance that would keep that force from breaking free."

"You're frightening me."

He halted under the shade of an oak. "I have to. It's too dangerous for you to go on believing what we experienced on Mount Sangre ten years ago was merely lightning during a sudden storm. There *was* a storm and, yes, lightning did strike the rock, lightning attracted by the surge of power from the force seeking to break free. Which it almost did, thanks to that foolish ceremony the four of us held. As it was, a small part of the evil escaped."

"Where did it go?"

"I wish I knew. But even the wisest among us, such as Grandfather, don't know enough. Like you, I was there when it happened and all I can tell you is that something, I have no idea what, prevented the entire force from bursting forth. If we'd faced the full strength of that force, we four might well be ten years dead."

I stood motionless, stunned by what Luis had said. I didn't want to believe a word of it and yet, to be honest, I'd felt the wrongness on Mount Sangre myself ten years ago and had always been afraid to admit the truth.

"Is that why you warned me and Tibbie to leave?" I asked finally. "Because Willa and I were a part of that ceremony?"

He nodded. "The four of us may be tainted. Tibbie isn't Willa, but she grew inside Willa for nine months. I can't say something dark passed from mother to child, but I can't be sure it didn't, either."

The spells—oh, God, the spells. Was that Tibbie's dark legacy from her birth mother?

"For the first time in ten years," he went on, "three of the four of us are here, close to Mount Sangre. And while the fourth is dead, her child is alive and here. The combination scares the hell out of me."

I bit my lip, determined to take Tibbie away as soon as possible. "Have you talked to Travis?" I asked.

"I tried to once but you know Travis. He took what I said as the joke of the century." Luis glanced at his watch. "Damn. I've got to get back to the office, but I'll see you sometime tonight."

I nodded and we walked rapidly toward the house. He stopped in the driveway beside his car, frowning. "I'm worried. I wish I didn't have to leave you."

I tried to smile. "You said that the other night— though maybe for a different reason."

He smiled one-sidedly. "I haven't forgotten." He started to reach for me when Tibbie hailed him, running up the driveway to join us.

"Luis! Are you going already? I was hoping you could stay and watch me ride. I'm lots better."

"Not today," he said. "Maybe this weekend, okay?"

"I guess doctors are mostly busy," she said.

"*Mostly*'s the right word."

"Maybe I won't be one when I grow up after all. Maybe I'll train horses instead."

"You've got a few years to decide," he said, opening his car door.

"Wait," Tibbie begged. "I forgot to ask what the Miwok word for goodbye is."

"We don't have one. In the old days, when a Miwok was ready to go he left without saying anything.

Over the years we learned to be polite and say 'adios' to the Californios, then 'goodbye' to the Americanos, but we still don't have a Miwok word for it.''

"Okay then, adios," she told him.

"Vaya con Dios," he said, his glance taking in both of us.

"That means 'go with God,'"', Tibbie said as we watched him drive away. "It's goodbye, too, but more like a blessing."

"Yes." I didn't tell her that I'd begun to believe we might be in dire need of a blessing.

Tibbie and I settled into the morning room with tall glasses of fresh-squeezed lemonade and a plate of the oatmeal-raisin cookies Delia had just finished baking.

"I'm afraid we'll have to leave sooner than I thought," I began.

Tibbie put down her half-eaten cookie. "How soon?"

"Well, like right away."

Tibbie blinked. "You mean before this weekend?"

"Yes."

Tears welled into her eyes. "But Luis said he'd watch me ride this weekend." She choked up. "Besides, I really, really want to go to the birthday party Mr. York is having for you. And I'll never get to see Soso again. Why do we have to leave now?" Her voice quivered on the last word.

I couldn't possibly tell her the truth, but I hated to lie, so I settled for half-truths. "We have to look for a new apartment in Santa Cruz and—"

"Why can't we go on living here? Bloodstone House belongs to you and Naranada's got schools I can go to."

"I need to work, remember? In a town this small, there's no job for personnel work like I do."

"You said your great-aunt left us some money besides the house. Can't we use that?"

"The money she left won't go much further than paying the taxes and upkeep on the house, plus Delia's and Jed's salaries for a couple of years." I hadn't expected to inherit a fortune, but Tibbie's question reminded me that Great-aunt Faith must have spent much of what she had on Luis's education. I still didn't understand her sudden spurt of benevolence toward a man she hadn't liked.

"Why can't you get money from selling the oranges and stuff from the groves?" Tibbie persisted.

"I'm afraid Great-aunt Faith didn't keep up the groves well enough for me to make enough for us to live on. Besides, I'd have to hire pickers and all. Don't argue, Tibbie. I'm sorry but we must leave."

She burst into tears. Jumping up from her chair, she ran sobbing from the room.

Sighing, I rose to follow her.

Tibbie, facedown on her bed, refused to be comforted. Even after I brought Diablo to her, she turned her face away from both me and the kitten and went on weeping as though her heart would break.

Wondering how to console her, I stood by the window looking at the bottlebrush below with hummingbirds darting among its bushy red flowers. Flowers as red as blood. We had to leave; there was no choice. But Tibbie was such a good kid. Disappointing her made me feel as though I'd turned into the Wicked Witch of the West.

"Mom," she said from behind me, tears in her voice, "don't you like me anymore?"

So then I cried, too.

In the end, we compromised. We'd stay over the weekend and leave the following Monday. And we'd invite Soso to come to Santa Cruz on a visit before school started.

Surely it was safe to stay here for those few days, I assured myself. Especially since I meant to be extra-cautious in watching over Tibbie. And, of course, neither of us would go near Mount Sangre. Not that we weren't too close already, here in Bloodstone House. But I'd be careful. Very, very careful.

In the evening, after Tibbie was asleep, I hung a circlet of old sleigh bells I'd strung on yarn over the outside of my closed door. I'd tested the bells and they rang loud enough for me to hear downstairs if the door was opened. Satisfied that if Tibbie had a spell she couldn't slip away without alerting me, I went down the back stairs to the kitchen for a cup of herb tea with Delia. Her nightcap, she called it.

"I'll be sorry to see you go and that's a fact," she told me. "I was kind of hoping you could see your way clear to stay on here with Tibbie. Perks up a person to have a child in the house, especially a smart and sweet little girl like she is. You, now, you were smart enough when you were small, but you weren't nothing like Tibbie."

I smiled. "I know I could be a pain. You and Great-aunt Faith had a lot to put up with the summers I was here."

"You weren't that bad. The trouble was Miss Faith wanted you to be like her—as if anyone could be. First Willa disappointed her, then you did. She never could understand that you can't make a child be what she ain't."

"I knew I'd disappointed her, but I didn't realize Willa had—not until the last anyway."

"Poor Willa. She tried to please everyone and wound up pleasing nobody, not even herself. Your Tibbie's not a bit like her. Talking about Willa reminds me. I asked Lucy Jennings if she'd heard Jack Norton might be back in town. She hadn't but she'll ask around. Lucy's related to half the county, so if he's here, she'll find out."

"If Jack was the prowler, I don't think he'll bother us again."

"What worries me is why in heaven's name he'd want that old owl medallion of Miss Faith's. Wasn't worth much from what I saw of the thing. I never could understand why Miss Faith fussed so over it."

I didn't want to talk about the medallion. "I'd like to stay here longer," I told Delia, "but it's impossible."

She nodded. "You got your reasons. Seems a shame about Tibbie, though. She does love it here. When Jed came in for his afternoon cup of coffee you should've heard her going on to him about the pony. Telling him to be sure to take good care of Misty just as though Jed ain't been around horses all his born days. Got a kick out of it, Jed did."

"Yes, Tibbie will miss living here. I'm glad you and Jed are able to stay on and take care of the place until I decide what to do with it."

"It's like my home, I been here so long. Likely you'll wind up selling to Travis York, being he wants it so bad. The Yorks always did covet Rolland property."

I wasn't so sure I wanted to sell to Travis. But perhaps, in the end, Delia would prove to be right. I certainly could never live here again. Nor did I dare take the chance that the place might someday belong to Tibbie. No, it must be sold.

"Well, it's past time for me to get these old bones of mine into bed." Delia rose from her chair and carried her cup to the sink. As she rinsed it under the tap, she said, "I'm glad you're not leaving before your birthday. I'm helping Tibbie with a surprise for you and she'd have been crushed if you decided to go sooner."

That accounted for some of Tibbie's upset, I thought. She thoroughly enjoyed surprising me. I was glad now that I'd decided to wait until the weekend because it would have been a shame to disrupt her plans. But we did have to leave. Nothing must happen to hurt her and if I could prevent it, nothing would.

At the back staircase, Delia paused. "It came to me last night about that cat's-eye ring you gave Willa—the one she lost. I got to wondering if the ring couldn't't've been in the hidey-hole with the medallion the thief took. I can't say Miss Faith ever forgave you for giving that ring away. If ever she found it she might've hid it, sure enough."

I looked at Delia defensively. "The ring wasn't my great-aunt's, but mine. Mine to keep or give away."

"I ain't blaming you, but I can't say the same for her. 'That cat's-eye stone is a talisman,' she kept saying. 'Valora has foolishly given her protection away.'"

Delia's quoting of my great-aunt's words raised the hair on my nape but I refused to be upset, reminding myself that in a few short days both my fears and Bloodstone House would be left behind.

"Willa mourned the ring's loss," I said. "If my great-aunt did find the ring, she should have given it back to Willa. But Willa died without the ring. Since no one has the slightest idea if Great-aunt Faith found it, we'll never know whether the ring was in the secret compartment or not.''

"Seems a shame not to know, don't it? But the grave keeps its secrets—there's a lot we'll never know. Good night, now.''

Thoughts of the ring plagued me as I sat in the library trying to read while I waited for Luis. Talisman or not, the cat's-eye hadn't protected Willa on Mount Sangre. I wondered how the ring had gotten lost on that dreadful night. I recalled seeing the stone glow in the light from Travis's black Halloween candle, so Willa had been wearing it during that hideous incantation.

Had her rapist stolen the ring? If Jack Norton was to blame, I felt anything was possible.

I wished the medallion had been destroyed like the book of incantations my great-aunt had burned. Who among my ancestors had that book and the medallion belonged to? I didn't want to believe Rollands had ever dabbled in witchcraft. I couldn't imagine Great-aunt Faith having any use for the dark arts. Not that her actions didn't sometimes surprise me. She had, after all, paid for Luis's medical education—I couldn't fathom why.

This transaction between her and Luis was gnawing at me when he arrived, but when he caught me in his arms as soon as the door was shut behind him, everything fled from my mind except his scent, his taste, his touch and the sweet fire of his embrace.

"Luis," I protested against his lips, "you make me so crazy I can't think."

"Thinking's not exactly what I have in mind."

"In mind?"

He laughed, pulling me closer. I clung to him, relishing his obvious need for me and at the same time rapidly succumbing to my own need for him. Our kiss deepened until we were swaying, locked together, intoxicated by passion.

"If we don't move soon," he murmured, "we'll be down and dirty on this damn parquet floor."

Somehow, arms around each other, we managed to stumble into the library and fall onto the leather couch. I retained barely enough sense to remember about the bells and tell him to leave the door open.

In feverish haste, we stripped off each other's clothes to lie flesh to flesh. Taking it slow, taking it nice and easy, savoring every moment was for second times around, not for now. I wanted to touch him everywhere, wanted him to caress me the same way, and yet I couldn't wait for him to become a part of me. I wanted, I needed everything, all of him.

It was hasty, it was desperate and it was ecstatically wonderful.

I don't know whether or not the second time would have been even better because, as I lay nestled in his arms, I remembered what had been troubling me when he arrived.

"Is it true my great-aunt gave you the money to go to premed and medical school?" I asked, belatedly realizing that my words sounded almost like an accusation.

He pulled away from me to look into my eyes. "It's true."

Somehow not wanting to be naked anymore, I eased back, reached for my oversize T-shirt and slid it on. "I didn't think she even liked you."

"She didn't." Luis stood up and began to dress.

Watching him, distracted by his dark good looks, I was tempted not to press the matter. But I couldn't let it rest. Luis wasn't denying it but he wasn't explaining, either. Why?

I put on the rest of my clothes and scrunched into one end of the couch. He sat at the opposite end and we stared at each other.

"Do you mind telling me what brought about her change of attitude?" I asked finally.

"She didn't change her attitude. We came to an agreement." His voice was flat, his face expressionless.

"Please explain." Because his behavior was making me apprehensive, I spoke more sharply than I meant to.

"In exchange for the money for my schooling, I signed an agreement never to see you again or try in any way to contact you."

I gaped at him, unable to believe my ears. "How could you?" I cried.

"Ten years ago you told me that you hoped you'd never set eyes on me again. You made it clear you didn't want any part of me. If I couldn't have you, why not agree to Faith Rolland's terms? I'd always wanted to be a doctor so I could help my people. Here was my chance. I took it."

I couldn't deny I'd said exactly that to him ten years ago, horrified and heartsick because of what had happened on Mount Sangre. I might have meant every word at the time—but people change. He hadn't bothered to find out if I had. Instead, he'd coldbloodedly signed me away in exchange for money.

"I can't believe you'd do such a thing," I said.

He shrugged. "Like I couldn't believe your great-aunt would go to such lengths to keep me away from you. I asked her how she could trust me to keep my part of the bargain. 'Your signature on this paper is my guarantee,' she'd told me. 'One glimpse of this and you'd be diminished beyond repair in the eyes of my idealistic grandniece. She would refuse to have anything to do with you. I mean to do everything in my power to keep the Rolland line pure, to keep it free of mixed blood. She's young, I'm buying her time to outgrow her fascination with you.'"

His dark eyes met mine without a trace of shame or apology, infuriating me. The words he'd muttered in his sleep on this very same couch two nights past echoed in my ears. *I kept to the bargain. Now it's ended.*

He'd been speaking to her, to Great-aunt Faith.

"As far as I'm concerned the bargain has *not* ended," I said coldly.

"Isn't it a little late for that?"

I was damned if I meant to agree. "So you waited until she died and then broke the agreement," I snapped.

"I didn't break it—you came back to Naranada."

"And if I hadn't? You mean you never intended to come and find me?" I knew I was being irrational, but I was too hurt to be reasonable.

"I never forgot you. How could I? But I was sure, after ten years, you didn't even remember my name."

I glared at him. "I wish I hadn't. I wish I'd never met you."

He shrugged again. "She was right about the idealism, it seems you haven't lost it. What the hell did you expect of me, Valora? I couldn't read your mind ten years ago any more than I can now. All I could hear were your words, and what they told me was to get lost.''

"But I didn't mean forever."

"I know that now. I didn't then."

Part of me wanted to understand how he felt, but my pride prevented me from trying. He hadn't cared enough was the only message that came through loud and clear.

"I'm leaving this coming Monday," I said, rising from the couch. "I don't expect we'll be seeing one another again."

He got up, too. "Then you're not going to Travis's party?"

"Of course I am!"

"Then you'll see me again."

His refusal to get upset was so infuriating I wanted to hit him. "You know what I meant. It's over. Done with. Finished."

He half smiled. "Somebody, maybe Grandfather's favorite, Yogi Berra, once said, 'It ain't over till it's over.' And it ain't. Not by a long shot."

Before I could come up with an appropriately scathing remark, he was striding from the library. By the time I reached the entry he was out the door and gone.

I clicked the locks into place with unnecessary force and marched to the stairs only to slump down despondently on the third from the bottom. I was throwing so many things away, discarding them as though they didn't matter. Luis. Bloodstone House.

Was I right or wrong?

CHAPTER TWELVE

There was no future in a relationship with Luis, I told myself the next morning after spending what was left of the night tossing and turning in my bed. None whatsoever. Even if I could bring myself to forgive him for his agreement with my great-aunt, I couldn't stay in Naranada. For Tibbie's sake, I didn't dare. And Luis, I knew, wouldn't leave.

He was the only Miwok doctor in the area and, as he was well aware, his people needed him here. He understood them as no doctor from the outside ever could.

As I showered I muttered, "Damn your noble soul, Luis. I know you wanted to help your people, but why did you have to fall into Great-aunt Faith's trap to finance your medical degree?"

There were government loans—especially for minorities—and, if we'd been together, I would have helped him. Didn't he realize that? He certainly hadn't bothered to find out how I felt before jumping at her offer.

I pulled on shorts and a T-shirt, still muttering to myself, doing my best to ignore the niggle of doubt at the back of my mind—would I really have been so eager to help him ten years ago? My first year at UCSC had been hectic. I'd barely gotten adjusted to college when Willa had arrived, penniless and pregnant. Left anguished and guilt stricken by her death, I'd also had a newborn baby on my hands.

Would I really have welcomed Luis with open arms at that time?

"Aren't you ever coming down to breakfast, Mom?" Tibbie called up the stairs.

As I stepped into the hall, I saw sunlight from my window slanting across to illuminate an oil portrait of Great-aunt Faith painted when she was in her twenties. It hung in this out-of-the-way spot because she'd never liked the result. Since the artist was well-known, she'd refused to dispose of it altogether.

I grimaced at the portrait's slight smile, a smile that suggested she knew she'd win every contest, every battle of wits. Then I remembered she hadn't always. She'd lost once to her very own sister. My grandmother Hope had married the man my great-aunt had wanted, the distant Rolland cousin that Great-aunt Faith had met at a party in San Francisco and invited to Naranada for a visit.

The early pictures I'd seen of my grandmother showed a sweet-faced girl with a pleasant smile. I could understand why a man of that time might prefer an easier-to-deal-with woman than my great-aunt must have been even then.

Had Great-aunt Faith's resentment persisted? Had it festered through the years so that she decided to make certain that I, a second-generation result of that marriage, would suffer as she had? Is that why she'd worked so hard to keep Luis and me apart?

I shook my head. It had nothing to do with the past. As she'd told Luis herself, she believed his heritage wasn't good enough for the Rollands.

The fact he was a Miwok meant nothing to me, but his signing the agreement with her did. I sighed and was about to go on when I noticed for the first time that the small earrings in the portrait looked like they were cat's-eye stones. I moved closer. Yes, definitely cat's-eye. I'd never seen her wear those earrings. Nor had they been among her jewelry she'd left me when she died. What had become of them?

Cat's-eye protects, she'd told Delia.

Protects against what? I wanted to dismiss the belief as superstition, but considering all the strange occurrences in the past weeks I found myself wishing I had those earrings to wear.

Put it from your mind, I advised myself, turning toward the back stairs. Why do you keep trying to make sense of a puzzle with so many pieces lacking?

Later, when Tibbie began practicing her piano lessons, Delia came into the dining room where I was studying another portrait of Great-aunt Faith, this one done when she was at least forty. Her hair was still the Rolland red, like mine, and the same smile was still in place, but the earrings were not the same.

"Lucy's not going to be working today or tomorrow," Delia said. "She came by real early to bring me a loaf of that good zucchini bread she makes and said her mother was sick. She brought news about Jack Norton, too. He's still in the navy. The last his cousin Ed heard from him was a postcard in June from Denmark, where his ship was in port. Ed told her when Jack joined the navy he said he wasn't never setting foot in this hick town again and as far as he knows, Jack ain't never been back."

Denmark in June. It wasn't impossible for a ship to reach the West Coast in a month. And Jack could have slipped into town without letting his cousin know. But I had to admit it was unlikely that either Jack or his ship was anywhere near California.

If Jack hadn't been the thief, who was? Who'd taken the owl medallion? And how could the thief have been aware of the secret hiding place?

"You don't look none too happy," Delia said. "I sort of favored Jack being the robber myself, but it sure looks like he couldn't've been."

"Do you think my great-aunt ever told anyone about her hiding place?" I asked.

Shaking her head, Delia glanced at the portrait. "You can see by her face she was one to keep secrets. Unless toward the last she got confused enough to let something slip. I ain't got no inkling who to, though. Not me, that's for sure. When Willa was still alive, she might've sneaked around and found out, she was inclined that way. But Willa's been dead longer than Miss Faith."

"Tibbie's got it into her head Diablo led the thief to the secret compartment but, of course, that's impossible, no matter how closely he resembles Great-aunt Faith's cat. Sombra might have known from following her mistress around, but how could a stray kitten know?"

"Don't forget them four feathers. Cats got keen noses—he might've smelled the feathers."

I supposed it was remotely possible. But that meant the thief would have to know not only about the medallion but about the feathers, and then decide the kitten might be a help. And he'd have to bring Diablo into the library—the kitten wouldn't have wandered in of his own accord.

Tibbie insisted Diablo had been afraid of the owl medallion and that was why he'd mistrusted the library originally. But how could a cat sense an object made of silver?

"How would the thief know there was a kitten in the house?" I asked.

"On account of Lucy gossiping, which she does. A whole lot of people in town probably heard Tibbie found a stray kitten that looked exactly like Miss Faith's cat."

I shook my head. "It's beyond my understanding. I don't like what's happening, it scares me. I'd leave tomorrow if I thought Tibbie would ever forgive me for going back on my word."

"Maybe the worst has come and gone already," Delia said.

"Let's hope so!" I spoke fervently, but I feared hoping wasn't enough. "I've had all I can take of missing rings, secret compartments and intruders."

"If you want to ask him, could be Jed might stay in the house nights till you leave. Since his wife died two years ago, he don't have nobody waiting at his place for him."

I smiled at Delia in thanks, feeling a bit better. "That's an excellent idea. I'll ask him right now."

"Tell him I can put a cot in the kitchen. That way he'd get to rest and still be right at hand if there's any trouble."

I went to the corral with Tibbie, and, while she put Misty through her paces, I spoke to Jed.

"Why, sure, be glad to," he told me. "Want me to bring my shotgun along? She's an old twelve-gauge, but she works fine."

About to say no, I nodded instead. If I was worried enough about the danger to ask Jed to guard the house, he might as well be armed.

Later I told Tibbie that Jed would be sleeping in the kitchen at night. "I don't think the thief will return," I added, not wanting to alarm her, "but it doesn't hurt to be careful."

Tibbie wasn't the least upset. "Why should the thief come back? He got what he wanted. But it'll be nice for Jed. I think he's kind of lonesome at home 'cause he lives by himself."

I, too, believed the intruder had found what he wanted, but who knew whether either of us was right?

"Delia will be all alone after we go," Tibbie said. "Maybe Jed could come and live at Bloodstone House all the time then. If he did, neither one of them would be by themselves."

Delia had been widowed two years after she was married—just before she came to work for Great-aunt Faith. Even though she'd chosen never to marry again, maybe she'd like having a man in the house—he'd be protection, as well as company.

"I guess I could ask Jed," I said.

"I still wish we didn't have to leave," she said wistfully. "I didn't get to do lots of things I wanted to—like climb Mount Sangre."

I stared at her. "But you did."

She made a face. "I was having one of my spells so that doesn't count. You know I don't remember what happens then."

"I know. Yet you did remember you were searching for Diablo when you came out of that spell you had the night the thief got in."

"That wasn't exactly like my other spells," she said. "It felt different 'cause I knew what I was looking for, kind of like Diablo was calling me. And then there was a kind of whispering in my head about the griffins on the fireplace."

Willa might have sneaked around and found out. Delia's words echoed in my mind, chilling me.

You've been listening to too many superstitions and too many myths, I told myself firmly. Willa is dead and her spirit or whatever did not appear and whisper to Tibbie.

Because I had no explanation of how Tibbie knew to twist the griffin's head didn't mean I had to believe in ghosts. For the first time in weeks I thought with longing of my ordered office in Santa Cruz where I worked as a computer analyst for the personnel department. There, a computer glitch was about as awful a calamity as I might expect and, tricky as they were, computer glitches always had a logical reason for occurring. They posed problems that could be solved.

I realized with a thrill of dread that I might never understand exactly what was going on here in Naranada.

"This last one wasn't quite so bad," Tibbie said, "'cause I remembered what happened. But I still don't like having spells. That Palo Alto doctor with the two last names and the gray beard said I might outgrow them, but I'm already nine years old. When will I?"

As always, when she needed reassurance about her affliction, I concealed my own heartache, determined she'd never know how anguished I felt.

"No matter how it seems to you," I said, "nine isn't all that old."

Tibbie rolled her eyes. "Next comes the lecture on how you thought you were all grown up when you were thirteen and then found out you weren't when you got into that mess—"

I laughed. "Okay, so you know everything I'm going to say by heart."

Tibbie shook her head. "I still don't understand how you could get in a stolen car with some guy you knew was a—what did grandma call him?—a hood."

"I didn't know the car was stolen," I protested. "All I wanted was to get a ride home because it was raining."

"A ride with a hood. Who was only fourteen so you must have known he couldn't have a driver's license."

"You sound like my mother."

"That's 'cause you told me the story enough times so I remember really well what Grandma said to you. And she was right."

I'd certainly succeeded in diverting Tibbie's attention. Grinning at her, I said, "If I promise not to do it again, can we drop the subject?"

"Sometimes you still do dippy things, Mom. And so do other grown-ups."

"Maybe it's because everyone stays a child at heart."

Tibbie sighed. "Kids get all the blame."

Jed moved into the house temporarily, saying he'd think about staying on after Tibbie and I left. Whether it was his presence there or not, the nights came and went with no sign of prowlers until, finally, Saturday dawned, hot and muggy.

"Jed said he saw thunderheads forming over the mountains," Delia told me at breakfast. "Likely enough a storm's heading our way."

"A thunderstorm you mean?" Tibbie asked. "With lightning and everything?"

Delia nodded.

"Wow!"

Living as she had all her life in Santa Cruz, where thunderstorms were rare, Tibbie had seen very few so the idea excited her.

"I hope Luis comes before the storm starts," Tibbie went on. "Otherwise he'll miss seeing me ride Misty."

After not hearing from Luis all week, and considering our unfriendly parting, I wasn't certain he'd remember his promise to Tibbie. "He might be too busy to get away at all," I cautioned.

"I guess. But Sunday he won't be."

Sunday I'd see Luis at Travis's party. Or would I? Maybe he wouldn't come to the party and I'd have to leave Naranada the Miwok way, without a goodbye. Perhaps that would be for the best.

"What's the matter, Mom?"

I blinked. "Nothing. Why?"

"You look sad."

"I'm a little tired, that's all." It was true enough. Though I'd had no more ominous dreams filled with cryptic messages from my great-aunt, neither had I slept well. I could keep from thinking about him during the day, but my nights were filled with images of Luis, memories of Luis. Luis, Luis, Luis.

Damn Luis!

He came in the late afternoon, on the edge of the storm, lightning crackling as he climbed the front steps, thunder booming when I let him in.

"I love thunderstorms," Tibbie told him excitedly. "I hardly ever get to see one."

"We'll watch from outside." He glanced at me for approval. Seeing my nod, he led the way to the morning room and the French doors opening onto the brick patio where the roof overhang offered protection from the rain.

For Tibbie's sake, I'd made no objection, even though the storm made me nervous. I really didn't relish standing with Luis and Tibbie on the bricks, dazzled by bolts of lightning and jolted by the rolling thunder.

"I think it'd be fun to dance barefoot on the lawn in the rain," Tibbie said.

"I don't," I told her. "What if you got hit by lightning?"

"I read in a book that lightning strikes the tallest thing near it and I'm little so it wouldn't hit me." She stared into the pouring rain and pointed to a towering Canary Island pine at the far end of the lawn. "That's where it will—"

Before she finished the sentence a brilliant flash momentarily blinded us as, with a sizzling crash, lightning slashed at the pine, the shriek of stricken wood intermingling with the booming thunder. I think Tibbie screamed. I know I did.

I gaped, breathing in the scent of scorched wood as I watched the tall tree, its thick trunk halved by the lightning strike, topple in two different directions. I don't know how long we stood without speaking, shaken by the violent death of the pine.

Luis broke the silence. "A bad omen."

"I didn't mean for it to happen," Tibbie said in a small voice.

"Don't be silly," I told Tibbie firmly. "Lightning doesn't strike according to your whim. You had nothing to do with it." Then I glared at Luis. "I've listened to enough superstitious nonsense. It's no more a bad omen than any other natural occurrence. I suppose next you'll be telling me the earthquake that demolished part of Santa Cruz a few years ago was to punish the wicked."

"I know as well as you do man doesn't control nature." Luis's tone was grim. "Miwoks have always known nature is more powerful than man and capricious, as well, making life dangerous. The bad omen was the tree splitting and falling two ways. To me and my people it means the decision can go either way—to good or to evil."

"What decision?" I demanded.

"I think you know."

He meant Mount Sangre, I realized, and the owl and the raven feather. Unlike old Westerns where the good guys wore white hats and the bad guys black hats, the feathers showed the reverse. Not wanting to discuss anything about Mount Sangre in front of Tibbie, I said, "It's time we went inside."

Delia and Jed, standing in the open French doors, looking at the demolished tree, stepped aside for us to enter.

"That was a close one, yes sirree," Jed commented.

"I've had my fill of that noisy carrying on," Delia said. "Thank heaven, the storm's letting up."

Tibbie remained unnaturally quiet. When Luis suggested that, since he couldn't watch her ride, maybe she'd like to play a piece for him on the piano, she agreed with no more than a nod.

After I tried and failed to turn on the lights in the music room, we discovered the electricity was off.

"I'll check the fuse box," Jed said when I told him, "but chances are a transformer got hit. If that's so, might be awhile before they get it fixed."

Leaving Tibbie with Luis, I went with Delia to the storeroom and brought two battery lanterns, several candles and matches into the music room where Luis and Tibbie stood at the window. They were whispering when I came in but immediately stopped when they saw me. I set one of the lanterns on the piano.

"Can't you light candles instead?" Tibbie asked. "They'd be more fun. You know, like the olden days."

"You can read the music better with the lantern," I told her.

"I know all my pieces by heart—I only need to see the keys."

Humoring her romantic spirit, I lit the four pink candles in the silver candelabra atop the piano and turned off the lantern.

The novelty of playing by candlelight animated her, dispersing the shock she'd obviously felt when lightning hit the very tree she was pointing to. By the end of "Anitra's Dance" she was showing off for Luis.

"We dance to that in my ballet class," she told him when she finished. "Madame Olga says I might never dance professionally but I do have natural talent. I'd show you but I need music and the radio won't work without electricity. Neither will the old record player."

Old record player was right. My great-aunt had never updated to stereo or even to hi-fi. But Tibbie's comment reminded me of something I'd entirely forgotten. There was an ancient windup phonograph in the attic.

"I think I can solve that problem," I said.

With Luis and me carrying the battery lanterns and Tibbie a flashlight, I led the way up the two flights of stairs.

"Are there bats up here?" Tibbie asked as we entered the attic.

"You didn't ask me that when I showed you the attic after we first arrived," I said.

"That was in the daytime so I didn't think about bats." Tibbie peered anxiously about the huge shadowed room with its sloping roofline.

Luis held up his lantern. "No bats," he announced after a moment.

Reassured, Tibbie followed me as I skirted trunks, old lamps and discarded furniture to reach the windup oak phonograph. I lifted the top, propped it open and checked to see if there was a needle on the playing head. Finding there was, I bent down and opened the cabinet underneath that held the old 78 RPM records. I chose one at random and placed it on the turntable.

"Wind it up," I ordered Luis, pointing to the metal arm attached to the phonograph's right side.

After he obeyed, I flicked the lever on and, when the record began to revolve, gently set the needle at the beginning. I opened the two small doors that concealed the speaker above the record cabinet and the music of Paul Whiteman and his Cliquot Club Eskimos shrilled tinnily into the attic.

"Why does it sound so weird?" Tibbie asked.

"This phonograph and the record, too, come from the early days of recorded music," I said. "People thought it was great at the time."

Luis, shuffling through the records, came up with a recording of "Anitra's Dance." He handed it to me before clearing a space so Tibbie could dance.

"Wait, I need my ballet slippers," she said, grabbing the flashlight and hurrying toward the stairs.

"What made you decide so quickly there weren't any bats up here?" I asked Luis.

He shrugged. "I didn't feel any."

The answer was far from satisfactory, but I decided to hope he was right and let it be. Laying "Anitra's Dance" aside, I put on another Paul Whiteman recording, a fox-trot, according to the label.

Luis again wound the phonograph, and, when the lively music began, bowed and asked, "May I have the pleasure of this dance?"

"Only if you know how to fox-trot, whatever that may be."

He caught my hand, put his other arm around my waist and we began gliding across the dusty attic floor. Though I was no more than a fair dancer, it was as though we were magically attuned, and I followed effortlessly as he led me through unfamiliar steps.

"Is this fox-trotting?" I asked, more to keep myself from falling under the spell of being in his arms than because I cared.

"A Miwok version."

"Does that mean you're faking it?"

"What's fake? We're keeping to the beat, aren't we?"

There was nothing fake about the way being close to him made me feel. I wanted to stay exactly where I was forever. As we circled the small space he'd cleared, he pulled me closer and closer until we were embracing rather than dancing. The music slowed as the phonograph began to run down and our steps slowed, too. His lips hovered close to mine.

The song finished with a flourish, but he didn't release me. The needle whirred ever more slowly around and around at the record's end while we gazed into each other's eyes, oblivious. How could I leave this man without leaving my heart behind, as well?

"That's the slowest slow dancing I ever saw," Tibbie commented. "Don't you know the music's stopped playing?"

I hadn't even been aware she'd returned.

Luis let me go. "We hadn't noticed," he told Tibbie, "but now that you mention it, I believe you're right. These old records are short-playing, that's for sure."

He smiled at her and she smiled back, conspirators' smiles, as though they knew something I didn't. What had they been whispering about in the music room?

"I'll put on 'Anitra's Dance,'" I said abruptly, and Luis hastened to wind the machine once more.

As I watched Tibbie dance, I took pleasure in her talent. She drifted lightly and gracefully across the unpainted boards, easily adapting to the different cadence of the recording.

The thought popped into my mind that Luis was equally graceful. He always had been. I remembered watching him when he worked for my great-aunt in the garden and marveling over the easy flow of his every movement. Like father, like daughter? Before the dark bud of suspicion burst into bloom, it occurred to me that Travis also had an athlete's natural grace.

And who knew, maybe Jack Norton did, too.

I sighed, no longer able to enjoy my daughter's dancing. No matter how I tried, the past couldn't be forgotten. What had happened ten years ago was destined to go on affecting my life indefinitely.

Light suddenly glowed through the open door at the foot of the attic stairs, signaling the return of electric power. A moment later, Luis's beeper sounded.

We trooped downstairs, the magic of the evening over. Forever, as far as I was concerned.

"Are you coming to Mr. York's party for Mom tomorrow?" Tibbie asked Luis as he prepared to leave.

"I wouldn't miss it," he told her.

"I bet it'll be fun," she said. "Mr. York said we'd have the time of our lives."

Luis's smile faltered and his expression turned grim as he glanced at me. I felt a premonitory frisson of fear slither along my spine as Luis's dour look triggered a recollection.

The time of your lives.

Travis had said it to Tibbie and me when he first brought up having this party, but I hadn't paid attention. Now I remembered those were the same words Travis had used ten years ago before he'd led the way up Mount Sangre.

CHAPTER THIRTEEN

By Sunday morning I'd convinced myself that Travis had meant nothing in particular by the words he'd used to describe the wonderful time he was sure we'd have at his party this evening. Though he'd been the instigator ten years ago, since coming back to Naranada I'd come to the conclusion that Travis had been the least affected of us all by what had happened on Mount Sangre, and probably rarely, if ever, thought about it. I might not have forgotten what he'd said to Willa, Luis and I before we climbed to the top, but he certainly had.

I'd supposed clear skies would follow yesterday's storm, but I was wrong. A hazy overcast partially obscured the sky, yet did nothing to prevent the sun's heat from coming through. It promised to be another hot, muggy day.

After breakfast Tibbie said she needed to help Delia and so wouldn't be riding Misty. I went upstairs to begin packing but, when I found myself growing more depressed with each garment I folded into a suitcase, I stopped and wandered up to the attic to make certain we'd left the phonograph and its contents in order.

Since the air-conditioning didn't include the attic, the heat under the roof was oppressive. I slipped the records we'd played into their sleeves, returned them to the cabinet and shut the lid of the phonograph. Before I left, I glanced around at the accumulated discards of generations of Rollands. I'd promised myself to go through everything up here this summer, but I'd never gotten around to doing so. And now it was too late.

If I sold the property, I'd have to come back and decide what to keep and what to sell, give away or trash—not only in the attic but throughout the entire house. I shook my head, not relishing the idea of ever returning. Of course, I didn't have to put the place on the market immediately. As long as Delia and Jed were willing to stay on, I could keep everything as it was. Maybe next year I'd have a different perspective.

One thing was sure—I wouldn't bring Tibbie with me when and if I returned to clear out the house.

Despite the heat, I found myself reluctant to leave the attic, lingering, drawn to the oddments my relatives had stored here. Lifting an old-fashioned garden party hat from an ornately carved mahogany rack, I shook the dust from the faded pink gauze and drooping cloth roses and set it on my head, peering into the wavy glass of an ancient gilt-framed mirror.

I blinked in disbelief as I stared at what seemed to be the image of the upstairs-hall portrait of Great-aunt Faith when she was young. Quickly whipping off the hat, I saw my own features, somewhat distorted by the old mirror. Did I actually resemble my great-aunt as a young woman, or had it been an optical illusion? I hoped I was imagining the faint scent of lily of the valley.

As I started to replace the hat on the rack, I noticed a small rose brocade purse hanging by a short gold-mesh strap from the wooden peg that had held the hat.

Wondering how I could have missed seeing it when I took the hat, I unhooked the strap of the purse from the peg before returning the hat to the rack.

The clasp of the purse was fused shut by the passage of time and it took a pair of scissors I found in a tattered sewing basket to pry the metal apart. Inside was a yellowing handkerchief with lace edging, a definite smell of lily of the valley and what looked like a silver coin.

On examination, it proved to be a medal commemorating the annexation of the Hawaiian Islands to the United States on July 7, 1898. Thinking Tibbie would be interested, I tucked the medal into my shorts pocket and was about to close the purse when my fingers felt something hard under the brocade. Puzzled, I felt around inside and discovered two lumps between the satin lining and the brocade.

With the scissors, I snipped a few stitches and then eased the hidden objects free, startled to find myself holding two cat's-eye gems. The missing earrings! They'd obviously been secreted under the lining of this purse—my great-aunt's, by the scent of it. Admiring their golden glow, I wondered why she'd hidden the earrings.

It then occurred to me that the earrings and the cat's-eye ring from my father's belongings, the ring I'd given to Willa, might have been meant to go together. The ring, I'd been told, had been handed down to my father when my grandmother Hope died. Hope's ring, Faith's earrings. Protection? Against what?

I slipped the earrings into my pocket with the medal, hung the purse on the rack and left the attic to resume packing.

By the time Tibbie came up to tell me lunch was being served in the morning room, I'd filled and closed one suitcase and the second was almost full. We walked together down the front staircase and, as we approached the morning room, she took my hand and told me I had to close my eyes. I obeyed and she led me the rest of the way.

"Now you can open your eyes," she said.

The morning room had been decorated with what appeared to be every flower in the garden from asters to zinnias. A pink ribbon with Happy Birthday in gilt letters was draped in front of the French doors, and a bouquet of pink balloons hung from the light fixture above the table.

The table, covered with a linen cloth, was set for two with my great-aunt's only-for-best, pink-flowered bone china, plus the ornate Rolland sterling flatware and delicate Austrian crystal.

"Heavens!" I cried, properly awed. "And me in my shorts."

"Well, if I'd asked you to dress up, you'd have suspected," Tibbie said. "I wanted you to be surprised."

"I certainly am. And impressed. Did you think this up all by yourself?"

Tibbie nodded. "Delia helped, though. And she's going to serve us 'cause she says that'll make it a real party. But I fixed some of the food. Wait'll you taste it!" She pulled out one of the chairs, saying, "Please be seated, Ms. Rolland."

We began with cold borscht, served with sour cream, then worked our way through finger sandwiches filled with either ham salad or cream cheese and olives, both favorites of mine. Pink lemonade was the beverage. When I declared I couldn't eat another bite, Delia whisked everything away and, after a few moments, brought in a chocolate-frosted cake gleaming with candles.

"There's twenty-eight of them," Tibbie informed me.

As the candles flickered and burned, Jed came in and the three of them sang "Happy Birthday" to me, then watched me blow out the candles—all twenty-eight—with one giant breath. No mean feat, considering how choked up I was over everyone's kindness and the trouble they'd all taken.

"Your wish is going to come true, Mom!" Tibbie cried.

As if what I wished for the most ever could.

"You and Jed sit down and share the cake with Tibbie and me," I said to Delia as I rose to cut it.

"Jed and me'll have ours in the kitchen," Delia said firmly and couldn't be dissuaded.

I cut two large pieces and handed the plates to her. "Thank you both for helping to make this my best birthday yet," I told them.

Left alone with Tibbie, I raised my glass of lemonade and said, "To the world's greatest daughter. May all the surprises she has in store for me be as pleasant as this one."

She giggled happily. "Hurry up and eat your cake," she said after a moment, "so you can open your presents."

I waved at the table. "I thought this was my present."

"There's more." Fidgeting impatiently until I swallowed the last bite of my serving of Delia's marvelous devil's food cake, Tibbie breathed a relieved sigh when I set down my fork. Ducking under the table, she brought up three wrapped presents and laid them in front of me.

"Luis left you one, too," she said, "but I can't give it to you until we come home from the party tonight 'cause I promised him I wouldn't.'"

I sat wondering what Luis's reason was. Why must I wait until this evening? What could he be giving me that he didn't want me to see until then? Finally Tibbie could wait no longer. She lifted the smallest of the presents and handed it to me.

Inside white tissue paper, I found the carving of a pony, the light wood polished until it gleamed. "What fine work," I said.

"It's from Jed. I told him you still loved Misty and so that's what the carving is. He's making me one of Diablo." Tibbie handed me a larger package. "This one's from Delia."

I unwrapped a lacy knit shawl in a beautiful shade of rose. "So that's why Delia hasn't been knitting in front of me." I held it up. "Isn't this gorgeous?"

Tibbie nodded, pushing the last present toward me.

"Since you're the only one left, this must be from you," I said.

"It's in a box, but you still have to open it carefully," she warned.

I took her words to heart, unwrapping the box so cautiously she twitched with impatience. When at last I opened the box she'd come to stand at my elbow.

"Why, Tibbie, how unusual," I said, first of all appreciating the meticulous handiwork that had gone into the seed picture she'd created for me. When I realized what she'd depicted I put an arm around her, hugging her to me. "It's the secret pool where we went with Luis and Soso, isn't it?"

She smiled her pleasure. "I was afraid you wouldn't recognize it."

"How could I miss? Here's the pool, there are the rocks and the tree—oh, Tibbie, you couldn't have given me anything I'd like more."

"Soso showed me how to plan the picture and Delia and Jed helped me find the right seeds, but I did it all myself. I wanted to remember the happiest day I ever had, there with you and Soso and Luis."

I fought back tears. I'd been happy there, too. For all I knew, happier than I'd ever be again.

"No matter how wonderful Travis's party is," I told Tibbie, "it won't compare to this one. Thank you." I kissed her on the cheek and let her go.

"I thought it was pretty great myself," she said.

I didn't remember what I'd found in the attic until evening, when I pulled off my shorts to shower before dressing for Travis's party. Removing the medal and the earrings, I laid them on my dressing table.

I'd chosen a white sleeveless cotton with satin gold and silver appliqué flowers decorating the full skirt. As I sat in front of the mirror brushing my hair into place, my gaze fell on the cat's-eye earrings. I picked one up, held it against my ear and nodded. Yes, they'd go with the dress.

I'd just finished putting on the second earring when Tibbie came in holding the barrette of carved coral she'd found in her room when she first arrived. It had been mine, left behind when I was a teenager. "This matches my dress but I can't get it in right," she said.

She picked up the medal as I drew a strand of her hair from either side of her face, pulled them to the back and affixed the barrette to hold the strands.

"1898," she said. "That was a really, really long time ago."

"I found it in the attic—you can keep it if you like."

"Thanks." She slipped the coin into the pocket of her cotton jersey dress, then examined her hairdo in the mirror. "Do you think it makes me look older?" she asked, turning her head this way and that.

I pretended to consider. "I'm not sure about older but I'd say that style becomes you. How about me—will I do?"

Smiling, she turned to study me. Her smile faded and her eyes glazed over. I tensed in alarm, fearing she was slipping into one of her spells.

"Tibbie!" I cried.

She blinked and focused on me. I sighed in relief. "What's the matter?" I asked.

"I'm not sure. I saw your earrings—you never used to have any like that—and something happened inside my head. It's gone now. I can't explain any better." She reached a tentative finger to touch one of the earrings.

"I found them in the attic, too," I told her. "They're the cat's-eye earrings my great-aunt is wearing in her portrait in the upstairs hall. If they bother you, I'll take them off."

"No, don't. I like the way they glow and they feel like they look. Warm."

A far-off rumble made me turn my face to the windows. "Was that thunder?"

Tibbie shook her head. "I think it was a jet."

"You're probably right. The weather feels heavy, though, as though a storm may be brewing."

She bit her lip. "Again? With thunder and lightning?"

"I thought you enjoyed thunderstorms?"

"Sort of, I guess, but—" She didn't go on.

Apparently she was still shaken by the lightning strike the day before and wasn't completely convinced the demise of the pine hadn't been her fault.

"We don't have to go to the party, we could stay home," I said.

"I want to go! I'm not scared of a storm."

"I hope you're not disappointed in Travis's party. Except for Luis, he didn't tell me who else he was inviting and it's quite likely no other kids will be there."

"I don't care. Mr. York invited me, it's your birthday party and I want to go." She scowled at me. "Don't you want to?"

I stood up and smoothed my skirt, realizing that if I were to be truthful, I'd have to admit that I didn't. But Tibbie had no knowledge of what had happened here on my birthday ten years ago and I hoped she never would know. "I'm getting a little old for birthday parties in my honor," I said lamely. "Especially two in one day."

"You're not thirty yet, Mom."

I smiled wryly, glad to know that in her eyes I was still two years away from being over the hill.

"Who do you like better," Tibbie asked suddenly, "Luis or Mr. York?"

"I like them both," I answered quickly, refusing to be trapped.

"Exactly the same?" she persisted.

"Why do you ask?"

She frowned. "Because of my dream last night, I guess. You know, Soso told me that Luis's real name is his last name. In Miwok it's hard to say and I couldn't get the word right but it means red-tailed hawk hunting. In my dream, you were lost in the hills somewhere and there was a coyote trailing you and a hawk flying over your head, only you couldn't see either one. I wasn't in the dream exactly but I was, kind of, 'cause I knew what you were thinking and all.

"You were scared 'cause you didn't know where you were and a storm was coming. You tried to hide in a sort of cave, but a rattlesnake was inside so you ran away. The rattlesnake came after you. Then the coyote ran up and turned into Mr. York and the hawk landed and turned into Luis. First Mr. York said he could show you the way home, but then Luis said that wasn't the right way and you'd never get home if he didn't show you."

"So what did I do?" I asked when she didn't go on.

"You couldn't make up your mind and the rattlesnake kept getting closer and closer. You didn't know about the rattlesnake, but both Mr. York and Luis did, and they each took hold of one of your arms and pulled in opposite directions and you screamed and screamed and I woke up."

I suppressed a shudder. "That was some scary dream."

"Yeah. I almost decided to get in bed with you, but I hugged Diablo instead and he started to purr. After that I felt okay and I went back to sleep. Do you think it was a real dream?"

Puzzled, I said, "I'm not sure what you mean. All dreams seem real when they're happening."

"Grandfather Running Fox told Soso and me that sometimes dreams are real and those kinds of dreams are warnings we should pay attention to. But he didn't say how to tell the difference, he said we'd have to learn that for ourselves."

Images from her dream—coyote, hawk and snake—circled ominously in my mind while I tried to reassure her. "Some people, like Running Fox, believe in omens. We—"

"You mean like Luis saying the pine falling was a bad omen?"

I paused, uncertain how to go on, somehow no longer sure of my own beliefs. A part of me was tempted to grab Tibbie, rush to the car with her and speed from Naranada this very minute, away from omens and superstitions and Mount Sangre.

I didn't, of course. I'd always prided myself on being completely rational and rational people behaved consistently. I'd said we'd leave tomorrow and so that's when we would. At the same time, I knew very well that much of what had happened since I'd returned to Bloodstone House was beyond my rational comprehension.

Deciding I really didn't know what to say to her at the moment, I procrastinated. "What you're asking is important and I have to think about it some more. Maybe for a couple of days or longer."

"That's okay. It's time to go to the party anyway."

I'd seldom felt less festive but I nodded. Travis's party was as good a way as any to bid farewell to Naranada. In the morning Tibbie and I would be safely away from bad omens and sinister portents.

I'd be leaving the problem of Luis behind, too, and I knew that was for the best. It didn't stop me from looking forward to seeing him at the party, though.

We drove over to Travis's, taking the long way around to save the springs on the car. When we parked, I was surprised to find no other cars. We must have been the first arrivals, because it was almost nine and Travis had specified eight-thirty.

He greeted us at the front door himself. "I'd begun to fear you weren't coming," he said as he ushered us in. "How charming you look, Tibbie." He took her hand and held it to his lips, making her giggle.

"Each year you're more beautiful, Val," he said, bending to kiss me. The kiss was so brief I barely felt his lips on mine. It was as though something had made him pull back abruptly.

Looking at him, I found he was staring at me. Automatically I ran a hand over my hair. "Is something wrong?"

"I was just admiring your earrings. New, are they?"

"They were Great-aunt Faith's."

He cocked his head, studying me. "The earrings are quite nice but I wonder if cat's-eye is truly your stone."

"It's not my birthstone, if that's what you mean. But you know I don't pay attention to such things."

"What I meant was, that with your green eyes, emeralds would be striking."

"If you get emerald earrings, Mom, may I have the cat's-eye ones?" Tibbie asked.

"If," I said absently, feeling uneasy, as though something important had happened and I'd missed its significance.

"Where is everyone?" I asked as he led the way into what seemed to be a combination sitting and dining room. Paneled in pickled wood and furnished comfortably, it welcomed us. The background music was so unobtrusive as to be practically unnoticeable.

He smiled ruefully. "I'm afraid I picked a bad evening for your party. Everyone I know is either in the mountains or at the beach." He glanced at his watch. "Luis should arrive at any moment. When he gets here, there'll be four of us. Not many, but an intimate gathering is often more enjoyable than a loud crowd. Don't you agree?"

"I don't disagree." I seated myself in one of the gold plush chairs and Tibbie leaned against my knees.

"I'd hoped to have other young people for Tibbie to meet," Travis said, "but they're all away with their parents."

"That's okay," she said.

"I knew you liked to ride," he went on, "and I remembered an old horse-racing game I used to play as a kid. Really old, my father's, in fact. It was made before the days of electronic marvels. I've set it up here." He motioned her over to a game table in the corner of the room and began demonstrating the game's intricacies.

Feeling strangely restless, I rose and walked to a large window where I gazed into the darkness, wishing Luis would hurry and get here. Lightning flickered in the night sky, too far away for me to hear the thunder.

"I'll open some champagne for us," Travis said from behind me.

"Please, not for me," I said, turning to face him. "I don't drink when I'm driving."

He smiled. "No problem, the coffee is made. I'm testing a mocha blend at the moment."

"I would like coffee, thanks."

Travis left the room and almost immediately returned, wheeling a glass-topped cart with not only coffee but a tempting array of petits fours and cookies.

"There's fruit punch in the pitcher for Tibbie," he said.

I didn't have the heart to tell him that she didn't much care for fruit punch.

As he served me, I realized his help must have the night off, which meant the three of us were alone in the house. I didn't know why that should make me nervous but it did.

Clicks and clankings came from Tibbie's corner where she concentrated on the game Travis had provided for her. I watched him carry a glass of punch to her along with a plate of cookies. Never mind that she probably wouldn't touch the punch, he was certainly being a good host. Age had improved him; I couldn't imagine nineteen-year-old Travis waiting on anyone. He would have expected them to serve him.

He settled into the chair next to me and raised his coffee cup. "To your birthday, Val. May we spend the next one together, as well."

"Thank you but I'm not sure we'll be able to," I said, all but positive we definitely would not. Still, I sipped my coffee to be polite. I found the flavoring—mocha, had he said?—rather bitter, so I added more sugar.

"Remember the summer a bunch of us drove up to Kings Canyon?" he asked.

I nodded, smiling. I'd been sixteen then. Corenna, Pat, Ron, Dutch and I had all piled into the York station wagon with Travis at the wheel for a picnic at Kings Canyon National Park. We'd had a wonderful time.

"Miss Faith blew her stack when I brought you home after dark," he said. "I don't think she ever did believe we had two flat tires on the way home."

"Well, it *was* almost midnight. I kept telling you to drop me off first but, no, you had to take everyone else home before me."

"Get rid of everyone else—what other way is there to be alone with your favorite girl?"

I smiled at him. "You always were a conniver, Travis."

"Who, me? Never! God knows I used to envy old Luis with his grounds job at Bloodstone House. He could be alone with you the moment you walked out the door."

"Not if my great-aunt was watching and she usually was."

Luis had never been a part of Travis's crowd. As a teenager, the only time I'd had a chance to talk to him was when he was working on the grounds.

While Travis went on reminiscing about some of the things we'd done in the summers when I visited Naranada, I gradually got the impression his heart wasn't in the conversation and that he was waiting for something.

But, of course, so was I. In fact, we both were probably waiting for the same person. Luis.

He refilled my coffee cup, though I'd barely finished half its contents. "Maybe I made a mistake with this blend," he said. "If you don't like it, I—"

"No, no, it's fine," I insisted, taking several unwanted swallows to prove my words.

Travis rose. "Excuse me a moment."

After he left the room I checked my watch. Nearly ten. Where *was* Luis? I really didn't feel I wanted to stay any longer but I hated to miss him.

Travis returned cupping something in his hand. I was taken aback when he knelt beside my chair and offered me what he held—a small purple velvet case.

"Happy birthday," he said softly.

I opened the case slowly, not knowing what to expect. Two sparkling green stones winked at me. Emeralds? They had to be, after what Travis had said.

"They're lovely earrings," I said truthfully. "But really, Travis—"

"Humor me," be begged. "Try them on."

"But I can't possibly—"

"Please?"

Though I intended to continue to refuse to accept such an expensive gift from him, it seemed discourteous not to do as he asked.

Reluctantly I eased the cat's-eye earrings off and laid them on the table beside me, then put on the emeralds. They felt cold against my earlobes.

"Perfect," he murmured.

For some reason I didn't want to see how they looked so I wasn't tempted to find a mirror. Instead, I raised my hand to remove them but he caught it, stopping me.

"I'll be terribly disappointed if you don't at least give me the pleasure of watching you wear them until you leave."

Though I didn't like being pressured, how could I refuse? I was trying to think of a tactful way when Tibbie walked toward us with such a strangely blank expression on her face that I forgot everything else. Before I could ask her if she was all right, she spoke.

"Mr. York, where's your bathroom?"

He rose and I relaxed while he told her, sure that she wasn't having a spell and that nothing more than embarrassment had caused her to look a bit odd. Or maybe it was my eyes, because Travis's face also seemed a bit blurry, as though I was getting drowsy. It would never do to fall asleep in this chair. I fumbled for my coffee cup and swallowed another mouthful.

Maybe we ought to leave now, before I grew any sleepier. Tibbie was in the bathroom; I'd wait until she returned and then we'd go. Not wanting to forget the cat's-eye earrings, I looked for them on the table but I didn't see them. Where had they gone? I tried to rise from my chair and found to my horror that I was strangely shaky.

Travis steadied me, asking, "Is something the matter?" Was there a note of triumph mingled with the concern in his voice?

I tried to focus on his face and thought fuzzily that he shouldn't be smiling, he should be worried about me. I certainly was.

"Luis!" I cried. "Where's Luis?"

Travis's voice seemed to come from very far away. "He's not here, Val, and he won't be coming. I sent old conscientious Luis on a wild-goose chase into the hills to treat an emergency that doesn't exist."

"But I—" I wanted to say that I needed Luis here. Now. But the words wouldn't come. I clung to Travis to prevent myself from falling into the suddenly spinning room.

As darkness closed in around me, my last coherent thought was that I'd been drugged.

CHAPTER FOURTEEN

I found myself in a malevolent darkness, surrounded by unseen dangers, uncertain of where I was and so confused I wasn't sure whether I stood on my feet or lay supine. I feared for myself but more for Tibbie. Where was she? I must find her before— Before what? Though I couldn't remember why, I knew she was in deadly peril.

I tried to call her name but, as in the worst of nightmares, I couldn't utter a sound. Or move. I wanted to believe I was dreaming, but something told me I was not.

Only once before had I seen such total, impenetrable darkness. Years ago, on Mount Sangre. I flinched at the recollection. But I wasn't on Mount Sangre, I was—where? Suddenly a streak of light appeared, revolving until it became a tunnel with a fox running through it toward me. The fox halted at the end of the tunnel, its glittering eyes transfixing me.

"I told you never to take anything offered you in a dream," it said. "I warned you no good would come of it." As it spoke, the fox's muzzle shortened, becoming the face of a wrinkled old man. Then light, fox, man and tunnel faded and disappeared.

Had I taken something offered in a dream? I seemed to remember the green fire of emeralds but not from a dream. Travis had given me emerald earrings for my

birthday. As a gift. *Beware of Greeks bearing gifts.*
Hadn't he once said that? I didn't accept the earrings;
I didn't want expensive presents from Travis. Still,
he'd asked me to put them on and I had. Was I wearing them now? I tried to lift my hand and failed.

Was it Travis bearing gifts I should beware of? If so,
why had he warned me? Warned me and laughed, his
idea of a joke. Was it a joke? Nothing made sense in
this horrible darkness.

Without warning, I heard my great-aunt's voice. "I
gave you four feathers in your dreams," she said, "but
you didn't heed my warning. And now it's your birthday, now it's too late."

My birthday. How old was I? I couldn't remember.
Not eighteen, I knew, because I'd been eighteen that
awful night on Mount Sangre. Years ago. How many?
Willa had died since then but not her daughter. Not
Tibbie. Tibbie was mine to love and keep safe. But
how could I keep her safe when I was trapped in this
darkness and didn't know where she was?

Luis. If only Luis would come. He'd help me, I
knew he would.

Luis is on a wild-goose chase. Who'd said those
words to me?

Luis wasn't here to help me. I was alone with no one
to rescue me from this dark waste where I was ma-
rooned, unable to speak or move, unable to protect
myself, much less Tibbie.

The fox face appeared again, shifting back and
forth from fox to old man. "Beware the thief who
carries darkness within him," it said, "for his coming
brings darkness and death."

I watched the fox man's face vanish, knowing I'd
heard the warning before but unable to recall where or

when. Was I already in the darkness brought by the thief? Who was the thief?

"I led you to those cat's-eye earrings to protect you," my great-aunt whispered in my ear. "You foolishly removed them. Removed your protection. I can't help you now."

I hadn't wanted to take them off but I had. To replace them with emeralds I didn't want. Why had Travis asked me to put on the emeralds? If only I could understand what was happening and where Tibbie was.

Other faint voices drifted to me, fading in and out as though from a radio station too distant to come in clearly.

Who are you? I tried to call. Please help me! I could feel my lips form the words but no sound emerged. My mind seemed a hopeless tangle, leaving me incapable of following any one thought to a conclusion. Instead, snippets of ideas, of memories, and of reason skittered at random through my head like water bugs on a pond, taking me nowhere.

Bat wings of panic fluttered inside me; I fought to conquer my overwhelming fear. If ever I was to discover a way to free myself from the darkness and find Tibbie, I had to set my mind in order, beginning with the answer to one question: Where was I? But the question had many parts.

First of all, was I standing or sitting or lying? I concentrated on awareness of my body. Though unable to move, I could feel hardness both under me and against my back, but the pressure was uneven. I decided I must be sitting rather than lying down. Sitting on a chair?

If so, the chair was extremely hard. And my legs seemed to be stretched out rather than bent at the knee. With great effort, I managed to shift my right hand. It slipped from my lap onto—what? My fingers told me dirt lay under my hand. I must be outdoors, sitting on the ground.

It flashed into my mind that I'd been at a party. My birthday party. Sunday night. At Travis's house. Tibbie had been with me. Where was she now? Why was I outside?

Be careful, I warned myself. Keep to the first question; don't ask others. Not yet. I knew I was outdoors. The next step was to determine exactly where.

The surface my back rested against was uneven and uncomfortable and hard as a rock. *A rock.* Fear clogged my breathing as an awful possibility shook me. The rock at the top of Mount Sangre. Suddenly and horribly, I knew exactly where I was.

Grimly I fought my terror. Panic would do nothing to help me, and more important, Tibbie.

I concentrated on what else I could sense and discovered flashes of muted light pulsing through the blackness. Were my eyes opened or closed? I couldn't be sure but, because I was in darkness, I decided they must be closed. If I'd been able to move my hand, I surely could open my eyes.

I did. It was still dark, but the softer darkness of night instead of profound blackness. Lightning flickering in the sky showed me I was seated on the ground, propped against rock, exactly as I'd thought. To my immense relief, Tibbie huddled against my left side. Thank God she was all right. I tried to say her name but only mumbled.

"Mom?" she whispered.

I longed to reassure her, to touch her, but I couldn't move.

"Are you awake, Val?" Travis asked from behind me and I realized he must be standing on the rock. He stepped down and stood in front of me. "Yes, I see that you are. Good. I want you to be aware of exactly what's going to happen. You deserve to suffer because this is all your fault."

My fault? What in God's name was he talking about? A confused jumble of impressions crowded into my mind—the party at his house, Tibbie leaving the room, my dizziness, the realization I'd been drugged....

Drugged! No wonder I was so helpless. But the drug must be wearing off or I wouldn't have roused.

"I've waited a long time for this," Travis said. "Ten years. None of it would have been necessary if you'd played Juliet to my Romeo the way you were meant to."

He was harping on that old theme again. I'd enjoyed his company when we were young, but I'd never wanted to be his Juliet.

"If you'd played your part," he went on as lightning flickered and flashed, "we'd be together as fate intended, but you were too blind to see what I visualized so clearly. You didn't seem to understand it had to be or that I'd never give up. When I read what was in that old book you found in your great-aunt's library ten years ago, I believed I'd found the solution, the way to unite us forever. Your stubbornness forced me to use the invocation. And it might have worked if Willa hadn't interfered."

I listened to him in growing horror. I'd realized he'd brought Tibbie and me to the top of Mount Sangre for some dreadful purpose, but I hadn't understood how obsessed he was with the Romeo-Juliet business.

Travis dropped to one knee in front of me in a ghastly travesty of a man proposing marriage. The lightning playing around us tinted his skin an eerie green, giving his face a sinister cast. He dangled something before me and I gasped when I recognized the owl medallion.

"You!" I croaked hoarsely, finally able to speak. "You're the thief!"

"The medallion was mine by right," he said, "but I lost it that night ten years ago and Miss Faith found it before I did. After she hid the medallion in her secret place, another might have given up, but not me. I've been searching all these years, searching Bloodstone House at night while everyone slept. That window latch in the library has been loose for a long, long time."

Travis had been the intruder. He'd only pretended to guard the house, pretended to chase a prowler.

"Why?" I asked.

"Really, Val, you're being very dense. Obviously because I needed the medallion to free the force."

A chill gripped me. Luis and Running Fox had spoken of the force within the rock I leaned against. An evil force.

"Evil," I warned. "There's evil in the rock."

Lightning illuminated his pitying smile. "You'll understand what it is when I control the power." He caressed the medallion. "Luck finally favored me. Your great-aunt's mind failed, she grew forgetful and began looking for the medallion herself, unable to recall where she'd hidden it. Watching her night after night, I narrowed the possible hiding places to the library. I was searching the room the night Miss Faith walked in and caught me. Fortunately, the shock was too much for her heart."

Fortunately? How could he be so callous? "You killed her," I accused.

"Spare me the drama—she was overdue to die. But I still didn't have a clue to where she'd hidden the medallion. Not until after you arrived. When I heard Tibbie say her kitten was afraid to go into the library because of the owl, at first I thought you'd discovered the medallion. Careful questioning convinced me you hadn't and so I devised a plan, using the kitten. I walked around the library holding him and when I came near the library griffins, he panicked. The damn little beast bit my finger to the bone trying to get away. Once I removed the medallion, I shut him inside the hole, hoping he'd suffocate for his sins."

Hearing Tibbie's muffled moan, and longing to offer comfort, I managed to raise my arm enough to lay it over her shoulders. If only my strength would return, we might stand a chance of escaping from Travis. What he said was terrifying, but I told myself as long as he merely talked and didn't act, there was a slim chance I'd recover enough to help Tibbie get away.

"You're frightening Tibbie," I said. "Please let her go."

"She's Willa's daughter. I need her."

"Why? She's only a child."

"Think back to ten years ago when you, Luis, Willa and I stood around this rock. I'd memorized a binding invocation from the spell book because I meant to bind you to me forever. At that time I knew nothing about the occult. Hell, I wasn't even sure the invocation would work. I'd set the ceremony on this rock up here only because of Mount Sangre's bloody history, not because I knew what was trapped in the rock."

"Evil," I whispered.

"Power," he corrected. "I followed the instructions carefully, pouring the cat's blood in a circle around the medallion as I chanted. I could feel tension building, building, darkness closed over us and then there was this tremendous explosion as the force burst from the rock. If it hadn't been for Willa's damn cat's-eye ring, the power would have entered me, the one who called it forth."

"Mom," Tibbie whispered.

I didn't answer, not wanting to call Travis's attention to her, still praying I'd find a way to help her escape.

"That's why I had to persuade you to take off your cat's-eye earrings," he said, "by pretending my grandmother's emerald earrings were your birthday gift from me. As they will be once we're married. Cat's-eye draws the force but also blocks it. Willa's ring drew the power into her, but then the cat's-eye flung most of the force back into the rock. A small portion escaped, entering me. I've studied the occult extensively since then and I realize if all the power had flowed into me without being channeled through Willa, I'd be ten years dead. In a sense, she saved my life."

"And almost died in the process," I said angrily. "I think the experience eventually did kill her."

He shrugged. "Willa wasn't strong enough to control even the minute part of the power she retained. I believe, though, some of it passed to Tibbie before she was born. I might have contributed a bit, too."

I was so upset by what he was saying that I almost missed the significance of his last few words. *He* contributed? The only way that could be true was if he was the one who raped Willa.

I stared at him in the now almost continuous lightning flashes and he must have seen the horrified comprehension on my face.

"I couldn't help myself. The power I'd taken in drove me," he said. "But I meant it to be you, not Willa. When I couldn't find you, I had no choice."

Speechless with mingled outrage and terror, I understood I'd never really known Travis. All I'd seen was his surface charm, the playful boyishness he showed to the world, a polished veneer that hid the murky depths lurking underneath. I prayed that Tibbie hadn't made sense of his words, that she didn't know what he'd revealed.

"You wouldn't want Tibbie harmed in any way, I'm sure," I said, hoping since he'd admitted he was her father, he had some feeling for her. "We're about to be caught in a storm. If she leaves now, maybe—"

"There's no storm coming," Travis said. "The force senses my presence, senses a chance to break free, and the force is what's attracting the lightning. Tibbie's presence is essential. Like Willa, she's a channel."

"But she's only a child!" I cried. "She'll be hurt. Remember what happened to Willa."

"I want the power freed," he said. "All the power. Tibbie will channel it into me. Her survival is immaterial."

How monstrous! What kind of a father would condemn his own daughter to death? He must be insane. I'd regained only a fraction of my strength, but Tibbie had to escape before he began his dreadful ceremony or she was doomed. I couldn't so much as stand up—how could I save her?

My arms and hands weren't as feeble as my legs so the only possibility I could think of was for me to grab him and hang on as long as I could, giving Tibbie the chance to flee down the hill. Preparing to lunge at him, I opened my mouth to shout, "Run, Tibbie!"

Before my words were out, Travis leaped to his feet, reached across me, grabbed Tibbie by the arm and yanked her toward him. "I've wasted enough time," he said, circling away from me around the stone. Frantic to keep Tibbie in view, I tried to rise, but my muscles were still mushy and I sagged against the rock. Squirming and twisting, I forced myself to turn until I was on my knees facing the rock, clutching it with my hands to keep from falling.

Travis stood across the rock from me, one arm around Tibbie's waist as he held her in front of him. One of her hands was cupped and, as lightning flashed, I thought something gleamed briefly through her fingers.

"You won't be afraid once I control the power," Travis told me. "Under its influence you'll be overjoyed to be my Juliet, you'll do whatever I ask and we'll both be happy. You and I will be together, the Yorks, the Rollands and our properties united, and Mount Sangre will be mine forever."

He was crazy. Mad. I cringed as I watched him raise the medallion to the lightning-lit heavens as he began the chant. The alien names hung malevolently in the heavy air, denying me breath until every inhalation became a struggle.

Still chanting, still holding Tibbie in front of him, Travis placed the medallion on the rock and reached into his pocket. Until I heard a weak squawk, I didn't recognize what he laid next to the medallion as his mother's little green-and-yellow parakeet. I heard the click of a clasp knife opening, then, with a quick stroke, he slashed off the bird's head. He grasped the twitching body and dribbled the parakeet's blood in a circle around the medallion.

Sickened, fearing for Tibbie, I pressed my forehead to the rock, no longer able to watch. Travis had thought of everything. He'd sent Luis into the hills so he couldn't possibly rescue us, he'd drugged me so I was still too weak to walk or fight, and Tibbie was only a child, frightened out of her wits. Escape was hopeless.

A rumble of thunder made me raise my head. With all the strange lightning, this was the first thunderclap. Was it possible Travis could be wrong about the storm? But, even if he was, I couldn't see how a storm would help Tibbie and me.

I clenched my fingers into the rock so desperately that I felt a chunk break away, its sharp edge jabbing my palm. A possible weapon? I hefted the chunk. Though no larger than a lime, it was jagged rather than round. I had a knack for throwing a ball and so I might be lucky enough to hit him. But the drug had sapped my strength—was I strong enough? And even if I hit him, would he be hurt enough for it to matter?

At that moment, I saw what I'd been dreading—a white feather drifting down toward the rock. Aware I had no time left, I gripped the jagged missile, drew back my arm, aimed at Travis's head and flung it as hard as I could.

Time seemed to stand still—the feather hanging in midair, the chunk of stone traveling toward Travis without reaching him—as with difficulty I gathered enough breath to call to Tibbie to flee when the chance came.

I didn't see Travis struck but I saw him stagger back, his grip on Tibbie loosening, and I knew I'd hit him. "Run, Tibbie!" I shouted.

She jerked free of him, racing away from the rock. For an instant I thought she might make it down the hill before he recovered. But all too soon Travis stumbled to his feet and rushed after her, both of them disappearing from view. I prayed she'd get away from him.

I slumped against the rock in disappointment when he reappeared, Tibbie hung over his shoulder like a sack of cattle feed. He said not a word as he resumed his position opposite me, sliding Tibbie down until she was in front of him, facing the rock. The frenzied lightning flashes, now followed by rolling booms of thunder, showed me a bloody gash on his right temple.

"Zariatnctmik, Etituamus, Almouzin," he intoned, beginning the invocation again. Belatedly I noticed that the white feather now rested inside the bloody circle on the owl medallion, its tip stained red.

The brooding, invisible menace, which hadn't quite dissipated during the pause in the ceremony, increased tenfold as he droned on. Darkness settled over the top of Mount Sangre, blotting out the lightning, cloaking me until I could no longer see anything. I despaired. Tibbie and I were lost. Even if, by some miracle, Luis were to arrive now, he'd be too late.

Travis's chanting seemed to echo in the darkness. My mind, numbed by terror, struggled to understand why the echoed words sounded different. I don't know how long it was before I realized I was hearing two male voices intoning separate chants, both in unfamiliar tongues.

Something brushed softly against my cheek. Involuntarily I reached up and found myself clutching a feather. From the owl? Horrified, I tried to throw the feather away but it clung to my fingers as though glued there. I huddled on the ground, fighting to keep from dissolving into panicked hysteria.

My heart pounded so loudly I thought I could feel its throbbing in my bones. Or was it thunder I heard? No, thunder boomed randomly and this was a rhythmical sound. Gradually I realized it wasn't my heart I heard and felt, it was drumbeats.

Travis had no drum. Where did the sound come from? Did I sense the evil force in the rock throbbing as it fought its way free? Whatever I heard, I feared no good would come of it. Tibbie and I were doomed.

CHAPTER FIFTEEN

The drum throbbed as I huddled, despairing, in the menacing darkness on top of Mount Sangre. I'd heard no drumbeats ten years ago, nor had there been two voices chanting. I raised my head, not hoping—for I was beyond hope—but to confront as best I could whatever horror came.

Light pierced the darkness. Not the brash flare of lightning but a soft golden glow. By the feeble light I saw that the feather I held so unwillingly in my hand was black, not white. A good omen? If only I could believe it was. But I could feel an ominous shudder in the rock as the force within gathered power, fighting to be free, and I feared it was too late for good omens, too late for anything or anyone to turn back the ancient evil locked inside.

As I clutched the feather, numb with dread, an eerie whistle joined the drumbeats, a whistle high and shrill, hurting my ears and so piercing that it shredded the unnatural darkness until once more I saw lightning flash above me in the night sky. The whistling trills wove through the chants of both Travis and the unknown.

I stared across the rock, searching for Tibbie, finding her still clasped in front of Travis. I saw no drum or drummer and nothing to account for the whistling. Thunder roared, momentarily eclipsing all other sound. As the echoes faded, without warning and so suddenly it seemed to materialize from the night itself, a strange and towering feathered figure, neither man nor bird, sprang onto the rock, spread mighty wings and began to dance, twirling in circles, kicking away the medallion, trampling the blood and the owl feather underfoot.

With a shout of rage, Travis flung Tibbie aside and leaped onto the rock, knife in hand, to grapple with the alien figure. Lightning streaked from all sides and great crashes of thunder rolled, reverberating from the nearby hills. Rain sluiced down.

As I struggled to rise, hands grasped mine, pulling me to my feet. At the same time I heard Tibbie's voice close by my side.

"Mom!" She flung herself at me, clinging, while whoever had come to my aid steadied us.

Lightning revealed a wrinkled old face, a face I recognized. I gaped at Running Fox, who wore nothing but a loincloth with the head of a fox set atop his own and a drum slung over his shoulder.

"Come," he urged, pulling at my arm.

I cast one fearful backward glance at the struggle on the rock. A searing, shattering crash shook the hilltop, then total darkness covered the rock, masking the two figures.

Leaning heavily on Running Fox and keeping one arm around Tibbie, I stumbled away from the rock and those who fought atop it. Travis and—who? Or was it what?

What I'd seen leap onto the rock was no mere man dressed in a raven-feathered cloak. Awe shivered through me.

Kuksu!

I must have whispered the name aloud because Running Fox echoed, "Kuksu. Come to save us all."

At the bottom of the hill, soaked through to the skin, we staggered into the shed for the meager shelter it provided from the rain.

"Where's Luis?" I gasped, sinking onto the ground, too weak to remain on my feet. Tibbie knelt beside me.

"Luis will come," Running Fox said, crouching in front of us and resting a hand on Tibbie's head. "Your heart is strong," he told her. "You helped by defying the evil with your amulet."

"I was scared," she said, her teeth chattering.

"The world is frightening," he agreed. "We who live here can only try to be brave."

I hugged Tibbie and she clung to me. "Who will win?" I whispered.

"The man borrows strength from the evil within the rock," Running Fox said, "but Kuksu, too, is strong."

Did he mean the battle could go either way? I thought of the pine trunk splitting and the halves falling in different directions and how Luis had called it a bad omen. I shuddered.

"Where *is* Luis?" I asked.

"He answered a false alarm," Running Fox said.

I recalled Travis telling me he'd sent Luis on a fake emergency call into the remote hills.

"How did you know we needed help?" I asked.

"The feathers showed me. You were given four in warning of peril to come. You found four more of the same feathers in a hiding place. Why? I asked myself. Two sets of four feathers each. Two sets, eight feathers. This evening Soso told me your twenty-eighth birthday was today and the meaning came clear. Death would stalk you tonight. When I realized the danger, I sent word to Luis."

"But how could you reach him if he was nowhere near a phone?"

"Luis and I share many things—blood, healing powers and a way to know when the other needs him in a hurry. A phone wasn't necessary."

As I tried to make sense of this, Tibbie spoke.

"Mr. York's not coming after us, is he?" she asked. "I'm afraid of him—he's a bad man."

"I examined Travis York's body," Luis said from the shed's doorway, startling both Tibbie and me. "He'll never come after anyone again, Tibbie. He's dead."

"And Kuksu?" Running Fox asked.

"Kuksu is gone." Luis crouched beside us. "Can you walk?" he asked.

"My mom can't," Tibbie answered. "At least not very good. I can."

"I will lead the child," Running Fox said.

Without another word, Luis scooped me into his arms. We left the shed, hurrying through the diminishing rain toward Bloodstone House, just as Luis and I and two others had done ten years ago. But now both Willa and Travis were dead.

Nestled against Luis, I closed my eyes, at the same time trying to close my mind to the horrors of the night. The terror was over; Tibbie and I were safe.

Jed let us in, then roused Delia. I could hardly stay awake as Delia helped both Tibbie and me into dry nightgowns. Tibbie climbed into bed with me, we were joined by Diablo and the last thing I remembered was hearing him purr.

No bad dreams troubled my rest, but I woke at dawn with a raging headache and a foul taste in my mouth—no doubt a hangover from the drug I'd been given. Tibbie got up, brought me aspirin and a glass of water and then crawled back into bed with me.

"Mom," she said, "does your head hurt too much to talk?"

"I can listen to you talk at least," I said.

She sat up, reached into my bedside drawer and took something out, holding it in her closed hand. "It wasn't really stealing," she said, "'cause he took what didn't belong to him."

Confused, I said, "You'll have to start from the beginning."

"I'm not sure what the beginning is. I guess maybe it all started before I was born, but I wasn't alive then so I'm not sure. Anyway, when I had those spells you always told me I used to say, 'Where is it?' after I went into them and then 'I can't find it,' just before I came to. Well, when I saw those cat's-eye earrings you had on last night, a voice whispered in my head, 'What you must find is like the earrings,' only I forgot the whisper right away so I couldn't tell you about it then.

"After we got to Mr. York's house and I started playing that game, the whisper came again. 'Like the earrings,' it said. 'Look in a box on the shelf in his closet.' This time I remembered what the whisper said. I couldn't ask you what to do 'cause he was talking to you and it kept whispering, 'Go!' until I knew I had to look. So I pretended about having to go to the bathroom."

I stared at her, not certain what to say.

"I found what I was supposed to and I took it," she went on, "but then when I came back, you were sort of sprawled in the chair like you were asleep, only I knew you couldn't be. Mr. York tried to make me drink that glass of fruit punch but I wouldn't 'cause I hate punch and it spilled all over the floor. Then he lied to me, saying he was taking us home. He drove his pickup to Mount Sangre instead and tied a rope around me so I had to follow while he carried you up to the top. I was really scared.''

I bit my lip, certain the terrible experience would scar her for life.

"I was glad when I heard you moan," she said, "'cause then I knew you weren't dead. I kept trying to tell you what I'd taken from his house but I never got the chance. So, anyway, here it is." She opened her hand.

I couldn't believe my eyes. The cat's-eye ring I'd given to Willa lay on her palm.

"The ring is what I was supposed to find all along," she said. "And I finally found it so now I won't have any more spells. Was it stealing, Mom?"

"No, Tibbie, you didn't steal the ring." With the turmoil raging inside me, I was amazed at how calm I sounded. Deciding she had to know part of the truth, I said, "The ring never belonged to Travis. He took it—stole it—from your birth mother. The ring is really yours."

After a long moment of silence, Tibbie smiled. "Maybe she was the one who told me where to find the ring."

Tears threatening, I said, "I'd like to think she was." And maybe, just maybe, now that she'd found the ring, Tibbie actually wouldn't have any more spells.

"Grandfather Running Fox says the ring is my amulet and it protected both you and me until Kuksu came." She slipped the ring onto her forefinger and then her thumb but it was too large for either. "I guess I'll have to wear it around my neck on a chain till I'm bigger."

"That sounds like a good idea."

"If your head's better, can we get up? I smell coffee so I know Delia's in the kitchen."

Glancing at the clock, I saw it wasn't yet seven, but I decided I wouldn't feel any worse on my feet than I did in bed. Besides, I desperately needed several cups of coffee before I'd be ready to answer any questions Tibbie might bring up about Travis and Mount Sangre. Remembering Jed was in the house, I slipped on my robe and slippers and ran a brush through my hair before we went down the back stairs.

"Mr. Fox is on the patio," Delia told me. "I fixed him breakfast and he ate it there. Seems he'd rather be outside than in."

"Running Fox is here?" I asked, surprised.

"The condition you were in last night," Delia said, "it's no wonder you didn't know that he and Dr. Redhawk slept in one of the guest rooms. Apparently the doctor got a call—he was gone when I got up at six. Mr. Fox was already sitting on the patio then."

"Let's eat on the patio," Tibbie said.

A short while later, she and I carried trays through the French doors and set them on the patio's umbrella table. Running Fox, wearing jeans and a blue shirt, crouched on the bricks in the sun, a small pack beside him.

"You're up early," I said.

"The birds and I, we rise to greet the sun when he comes from the east to bring light to a new day," he said.

"Come and eat with us," Tibbie invited. "There's an extra cup of coffee and lots of cinnamon rolls."

"Thank you," Running Fox said, getting up and joining us. "I'm not often lucky enough to have a second breakfast."

Here in the pleasant bright warmth of morning, I might have believed the horrors of the night before had been a bad dream—if my still-throbbing head hadn't reminded me of what had occurred.

"Is Mr. York really dead?" Tibbie asked, coming directly to the heart of the matter while I was wondering how to begin.

Running Fox nodded. "Luis arranged for his body to be taken off Mount Sangre." His wise, shrewd eyes held mine as he said, "Travis York was alone on the hill when he was struck by lightning during last night's storm."

"But—" Tibbie began.

"Luis is trying to spare us having to answer questions about last night," I told her firmly. "Do you really want to try to explain what happened? Explain to strangers?"

She shook her head.

"The truth is that Travis York *was* killed by lightning," Running Fox said. "Why is it necessary to involve others?"

"I guess nobody'd believe about Kuksu anyway," Tibbie said. She caught sight of Jed spraying the roses and slid from her chair with a hasty, "Excuse me, I need to talk to Jed about Misty."

"Luis spoke to Mrs. Koski and Jed O'Neill last night," Running Fox said as she ran off. "They agreed not to mention anything about you and Tibbie."

"Thank you."

"It's Luis's doing, not mine. He left early, called to the hospital, but I stayed here until you woke because I must tell you all is not good. We have more work to do. Tibbie's yet a child so I didn't speak in front of her, but I say to you the evil is still there, still waiting in the rock on Mount Sangre."

I clenched my hands around my coffee cup, not wanting to listen, wanting the fear to be over and done with.

"I dreamed last night," he went on. "In my dream, Fox, my spirit animal, came to me and showed me what must be done. The soil of earth itself will protect us. We must cover the rock with many layers of the earth's protective soil. Since, according to the laws of this country, you, and not my people, have the right to Mount Sangre, it's up to you."

"I'm willing to help, but will it work?"

"Yes." The old shaman spoke softly, without emphasis, but with complete conviction in his voice. Several weeks ago, I wouldn't have believed him. I'd grown wiser.

"How much dirt will be needed?" I asked.

"Enough to cover the rock many feet deep."

I realized getting the equipment needed to haul and dump that much dirt up the steep slope of Mount Sangre would be expensive but I didn't care. Because of Running Fox, Tibbie was alive. I was alive. If he said burying the rock would protect us and others from the evil trapped within, I'd gladly spend every cent I possessed to do it.

"I'll arrange for the dumping as soon as possible."

"Good." He finished his coffee and rose, obviously preparing to leave.

"Wait," I cried. "What about—about Kuksu?"

Running Fox shrugged. "Luis summoned him. He came."

I stared at him. "Luis? I thought *you* summoned Kuksu."

"I'm too old. Kuksu needs to use the agility of a younger man. I helped by drumming, that's all I did."

I struggled to interpret what he meant, finally asking, "Are you saying the feathered figure who leaped onto the rock was Luis?"

"Kuksu challenged the evil. Kuksu was victorious."

"But where was Luis, then? I didn't see him."

"Luis was there on the rock and yet not there."

I pressed both hands to my aching head. "I don't understand."

"It's hard for you because you aren't one of us. I'll try to explain, but what I tell you is only a part of the truth. Luis as a man couldn't have vanquished Travis York, because Travis had taken in some of the evil. He was more than a man. So Luis invoked Kuksu. He became Kuksu for the time it took to conquer the evil within Travis. Kuksu called down the thunder spirits, lightning struck the rock and those who fought on the rock. Kuksu survived. When he was no longer needed, he disappeared. Luis was then himself again."

"You're saying Luis was Kuksu?"

"I warned you it was difficult. You'd be closer to the truth to say Kuksu was Luis, but that isn't quite right, either. Accept what you saw and don't try to understand."

I thought of the larger-than-life feathered figure who danced on the rock, spreading enormous wings, and I shivered.

"Accept Luis," Running Fox said. "Accept him as he is, accept him if you can. For you are the woman he wants."

I watched him pick up the small pack he'd left on the bricks and walk into the sunlight, striding away with the gait of a much younger man.

Accept Luis? He was already a part of me and he always would be. But that didn't mean we had a future together. Tibbie and I wouldn't be leaving Naranada today as I'd planned. Whether I wished to or not, I must attend Travis's funeral. And arrange for the rock to be buried under many cubic yards of dirt.

I walked into the yard and stared up at Mount Sangre, still feeling the uneasiness and fear it had evoked in me ever since the first awful ceremony at its summit. I could never live in the shadow of Mount Sangre. Once everything was attended to, I'd leave.

A week later, I stood in the yard once more, this time with Tibbie beside me, both of us watching the last backhoe ease down the steep slope of Mount Sangre. The top of the hill was thickly covered with dirt, so deep that Jed had announced his intention of planting seedling trees at the summit—live oak, he thought—along with the shrubs and grass I'd arranged to have put in so there'd be roots to keep the dirt from washing away.

"It's gone, isn't it, Mom?" Tibbie asked.

I thought she meant the backhoe. "Not quite, but almost. If it doesn't topple over on the way down."

She frowned at me. "I'm talking about the bad feeling. I didn't like to look at Mount Sangre after that night. But now I don't mind. It's just another hill."

Was she right? I stared up, waiting for the familiar thrust of fear to stab through me. Nothing happened.

"Like Grandfather Running Fox said," Tibbie told me, "the badness got buried the way Mr. York did."

I'd tried not to think of Travis at all, not even at the funeral.

"I think a piece of the bad got into Mr. York," Tibbie went on, "and that's why he did those awful things."

It might be true. Travis himself had said some of the dark force had entered him ten years ago. I decided I'd rather believe he was driven to his terrible acts than think he was himself when he planned to kill his own daughter and enslave me.

At least he'd finally found peace in death.

Strangely, either because I'd at last put Travis to rest in my own mind or because the evil on Mount Sangre was now buried too deep to be felt, my heart lightened as though a shadow had been lifted from me.

I smiled at Tibbie. "Did I ever happen to mention that you are one smart kid?"

She started to grin but almost immediately looked stricken. "Oh, no!" she cried. "How could I forget? Luis'll be mad at me forever."

Before I could ask her what was wrong, she dashed toward the house. I followed more slowly. By the time I reached the entry, I saw her coming out of the library with something in her hand.

"I hid it in the secret place," she said, "'cause I didn't think you'd ever look there. But then I forgot about giving it to you like I was supposed to." She handed me a small, thin packet wrapped in blue tissue paper. "It's your birthday present from Luis."

I remembered now she'd mentioned the present, but the horrible night of my birthday had driven the memory from my mind. "I don't blame you for forgetting," I said.

She rolled her eyes. "But I *promised* Luis."

I peeled back the paper and found myself looking at a small account book. A bank book. Frowning in puzzlement, I opened it. My name was written there and below it ITF, in trust for, Tabitha Faith Rolland.

The entries showed money paid into the account, beginning with very small amounts nine years ago to large amounts the past several years. I stared at the figures for a long time, trying to make sense of them.

"Luis said that after you opened the present I was supposed to tell you he'd paid his debt," Tibbie said.

And then I understood. Luis had known I'd never accept a return of the money my great-aunt had given him and so he'd set up the account for Tibbie. I looked again at those small early entries and realized he must have worked while he went to school in order to start the account. And I knew it wasn't the monetary debt that had bothered him—after all, it hadn't been a loan.

I saw now that from the moment he'd signed the agreement, he'd been determined to cancel it in the only way he could think of—by repaying the money. Not to me but to Willa's daughter. No one could bring Willa back to life, but I'd adopted her child and he could offer that child some financial security.

Tears in my eyes, I cradled the book between my closed hands, lost in a reverie, imagining Luis depriving himself to put money into the account. I don't know how long I stood there before Tibbie's voice brought me back to the present.

"Just tell him my mom liked her present," Tibbie was saying into the phone and I realized she must be talking to Luis's receptionist.

I'd seen Luis briefly at Travis's funeral, but he hadn't called or come by since. Would he now?

The day passed slowly. Finally dinner was over, eventually Tibbie went to bed and there still had been no word from Luis.

Restless, I left the house and walked through the moonlight to the gazebo, no longer afraid of the night or of the constant presence of Mount Sangre. I was safe but I was also alone.

Like all July nights in Naranada, it was warm, the breeze soft and jasmine scented. Fireflies twinkled in the shrubbery like fallen stars. I sat on the seat and gazed at the moon, riding high and almost full. Smiling a bit sadly, I thought of my seventeen-year-old fantasy of being the most beautiful, desirable woman in the world. I knew better now.

Luis, though, was everything I'd always imagined my dream lover would be, that and more. How could I possibly have known at seventeen the deep soul-wrenching passion I'd find in his arms?

"I knew I'd find you waiting here for me," Luis said from the steps of the gazebo.

This time I didn't deny it. Rising, I drifted to the railing, where he joined me.

"Tibbie's message said you liked my present," he said.

"She didn't remember to give it to me until today but, yes, I understood the meaning." I turned to him. "I'm sorry I didn't try to understand sooner."

The moonlight glowed in his dark eyes. "I wanted you from the first," he said softly, "and I wanted you forever. I've never changed my mind." He took my hands, holding them over his heart. "I love you."

"Oh, Luis, I've been so afraid to love you, but I do, I can't help myself."

"Then stay. Stay in Naranada and marry me."

I opened my mouth to remind him I couldn't, but I suddenly realized the reasons why I had to leave had all vanished. The shadows were gone from Bloodstone House; Tibbie and I were safe here. With Luis and, eventually, Soso, we'd make the old house a home. With time and Luis's help, I could and I would make the Rolland groves productive again.

"Yes," I murmured. "Oh, yes."

He started to pull me into his arms, then paused with his lips close to mine. "Tibbie will be pleased. She told me the night the electricity went off that she thought you and I ought to get married."

"If I know her, she'll be convinced this is all her idea."

As I spoke, something drifted between us, brushing my lips. I drew back, plucking it from the air. "A feather!" I cried, suddenly fearful.

Luis took it from me to study, then smiled. "Nothing to worry about, it's a feather from a red-tailed hawk. The best omen we could hope for."

I wondered if Hawk was his spirit animal as Fox was his grandfather's, but then he caught me in his arms and kissed me and nothing else mattered. I loved this man who held me; I accepted all of him—ancestry, beliefs and whatever else he might surprise me with in the future. I loved Luis and I always would.

*   *   *   *   *

Available in May from
Silhouette Shadows

FLASHBACK
by Terri Herrington

PROLOGUE

She was gone.

Marcus Stephens stared at the space where she'd sat just moments ago, gazing at him with tragic hope in her eyes, touching his hand with tentative certainty, offering him a precarious balance that he hadn't expected at this point in his life. Then she had slipped through his fingers, disappeared into thin air. . . .

Was she a ghost? he asked himself. Could he have held a ghost the way he'd held her last night? Could she have wept in his arms and clung to him as if she'd spent a lifetime looking for him? Would a ghost have had a fever so violent that he'd had to pack her in ice?

But if not a ghost, then *what* was she . . . *who* was she . . . and more important, *why* was she?

Could it be true, what she had tried to tell him last night? The thing about a camera and crossing lifetimes? No, it couldn't be, he told himself again. She had been hallucinating, babbling. There was no sense to be made of any of it.

She was a blessing that had been sent to divert his attention from the self-destruction he'd been contemplating. Or, she was a curse to further punish him for his sins.

Either way, she had been here, and now she was gone. Another secret to hide from the world. Another black spot on the soul he could never cleanse.

But in the throes of his dispair, a ray of hope pene-
trated the void in his heart. Maybe she would come
back from whatever black hole she had fallen. Maybe
he'd get the chance to find out, once and for all, if he
was as mad as he thought, or if she had really existed
for a moment.

It had been a long time since he'd bowed his head,
dropped to his knees and confronted the deity he felt
he'd betrayed. As he did it now, he did it with trepi-
dation, feeling humiliation and a great deal of shame.
Facing God with his bag of sins was more than he'd
been prepared to do, but some burdens were just too
heavy to bear alone. The fleeting thought of sharing
it with someone who may have been merely a figment
of his imagination only made him feel more alone. In
just a few hours, she had gotten under his skin, had
changed something in his life, had brought something
to him that he'd needed more than air itself. Why
couldn't she be real?

He knew why. It was his term in hell, and he'd
earned the sear of every flame that engulfed his life.
Still, if there was just a chance...

*This isn't my time. I've traveled back. I'm not
making this up, Marcus. You've got to believe me....*

What if she hadn't been hallucinating? What if he
wasn't mad? What if there was a chance—just a
chance—that she had been telling the truth, that she
had traveled here through some medium he couldn't
understand? What if she could do it again and come
back to him?

What if she couldn't?

Dread washed over him, making him feel more dis-
mal than he'd ever felt before. Despair wasn't some-

thing that got easier with experience. And this was a trauma he couldn't walk away from.

She had gotten to him, deep down where he needed her the most, and he determined, right there as he knelt on his knees, his head bowed, that he would wait for her for as long as it took.

He would find her again, even if he had to grow old to do it.

A romantic collection that
will touch your heart....

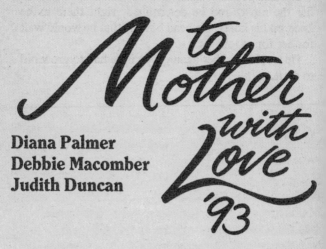

to Mother with Love '93

Diana Palmer
Debbie Macomber
Judith Duncan

As part of your annual tribute to
motherhood, join three of Silhouette's
best-loved authors as they celebrate the
joy of one of our most precious gifts—
mothers.

Available in May at your favorite retail outlet.

Only from **Silhouette**®

—where passion lives.

Fifty red-blooded, white-hot, true-blue hunks from every State in the Union!

Beginning in May, look for MEN: MADE IN AMERICA! Written by some of our most popular authors, these stories feature fifty of the strongest, sexiest men, each from a different state in the union! Favorite stories by such bestsellers as Debbie Macomber, Jayne Ann Krentz, Mary Lynn Baxter, Barbara Delinsky and many, many more!

Plus, you can receive a FREE gift, just for enjoying these special stories!

You won't be able to resist MEN: MADE IN AMERICA!

Two titles available every other month at your favorite retail outlet.

MEN-G